Redeemed by the Blood of the Lamb

By

Joan Byrd

Deep Indigo Books
Published by Indigo Sea Press
Winston-Salem

Deep Indigo Books
Indigo Sea Press
302 Ricks Drive
Winston-Salem, NC 27103

Copyright 2024 by Joan Byrd
All rights reserved, including the right of reproduction in
whole or part in any format.
First Deep Indigo Books edition published
September, 2024
Deep Indigo Books, Moon Sailor and all production design
are trademarks of Indigo Sea Press, used under license.

For information regarding bulk purchases of this book,
digital purchase and special discounts, please contact the publisher
at indigoseapress@gmail.com

Cover Design by Pan Morelli
Manufactured in the United States of America
ISBN 978-1-63066-608-8

Dedication

I dedicate *Redeemed by the Blood of the Lamb* to one of our dearest friends, Jerry Murdock, who saw the clouds of earth open and left us to walk into the arms of Jesus. I miss his laugh and listening to him and Ray, my husband, speak about happy memories at the children's home where they grew up.

Throughout our lifetime, we are blessed to meet people who make an instant impact on us, just by being themselves. One such person was Jerry Murdock. A great person with an unconditional love for everyone he met. There was a sweet gentleness that he possessed when around his family or close friends. Jerry was also a man of strong character and special abilities. Those personal qualities led him into starting a multimillion dollar company.

This warm-gentleman did not grow up in a wealthy family. Like most families living in the Depression, the Murdocks large family found themselves in need of help. So the four youngest Murdock brothers were placed in the Methodist Children's Home. Jerry, along with his older brother Sam and younger twin brothers Gilmer and Graham, spent most of their childhood with hundreds of other brothers and sisters. Back in the 40s, 50s and even 60s, children were taught how to work on the farm, which taught both boys and girls skills they would need later in life, when they left us as adults.

It was at one of the children's home reunions I met Jerry and Graham and Sam, and now years later, I still count them, plus Gilmer and their loving wives as some of my closest friends.

Jerry Murdock has one of the most giving hearts I know and along with his Joan, Jerry's wife and partner and my dear friend, they have helped countless people as well as organizations. The Children's Home has a special song they have sung since childhood. It goes: "We're the girls and boys from the Children's Home and a merry band are we. We work and we play and we're happy all the day, as girls boys should be. I'm proud of my home, is my home proud of me. What she needs is girls and boys trained in loyalty. When we work, when we play, with our fellow man, good citizens we will be for I am proud I am proud of the children's home and I'll make her proud of me."

I can assure you, my good friend Jerry, if you're listening from heaven, you were a better than good citizen. When you worked, you helped create a lot of jobs for hard working families. When you played, when you spent some personal time with your wife and children or enjoy spending time with friends, and all those moments your pure heart reached out to give, you showed love.

Jerry never forgot where he came from and he was proud of the home he grew up in and never stopped loving it or the family he called his brothers and sisters. His giving heart gave so the children's home memories would last for years to come, God willing. And yes, Jerry, your home is very proud of the little boy that left with almost nothing to become the man you became. I know without a doubt, our Lord greeted you in heaven with well done my good and faithful servant. We love you, we miss you and we will see you soon.

—Joan Byrd

CHAPTER 1

Jeremiah Mitchell stared out at the rising waves, rolling to a gentle crest before crashing forward into a rushing sound making an aggressive forceful advancement toward the beach. As soon as one wave ended in a silent retreat, another wave mounted its crest to repeat the rapid advancement toward him all over again. The thirty-year-old minister had waited for the beach to be vacant of beach goers and he knew he would be watching the setting sun alone, giving him time to reflect on his life, especially the last few days. The tired man could sympathize with the gentle retreating water that once felt strong and alive. Perhaps, he thought, the ocean waves were merely mocking him. The man of God who seem to be getting nowhere, making one step forward only to find himself getting knocked back twice and with no hope ahead.

After Jeremiah received his final test results from his doctor and good friend, Bennett Wells, he just couldn't face all the cheerful faces from Messiah Methodist Church and preach the service of Lent, not after getting a death sentence with no chance of being healed. The young preacher knew he could count on his other friend, Reverend Mason, to fill in for him without going into the reason he wouldn't be available. He used to find joy running on the beach in the mornings, just as the sun was rising, but there was no reason for him to run anymore. He was dying and it seem foolish and a waste of precious time, when there was only one thing he had hoped to do before he left this earth for heaven. Suddenly, the young minister was desperate to fulfill that one wish and he was afraid his chances of finding an opening left this late in the season. Most Holy Land Tours were sold out by the first of the year and the week he had longed for now seemed out of reach.

The loving preacher's thought turned to his church members, all of which loved their young minister who preached the gospel from his heart, with no planned sermons in front of him. Jeremiah had always been there for them, in sickness, at the death of a love one, or many happy occasions, such as performing a wedding ceremony. Many of the single ladies gave him the eye, but the handsome young bachelor had not found the right girl and now it was too late to know what being in love felt like.

"How can I tell all those beautiful Christians I have a rare, untreatable condition that has affected my blood from producing enough to remain alive. It has become extremely thin and without the normal amount I need to protect my vital organs and my skin, the slightest scrape will cause me to bleed uncontrollably." He watched the sky grow red as the sun drifted further down behind him. "If only Ben would have had a different outcome.

DOCTOR BENNETT WELL'S OFFICE: Earlier

"Doc, you said this condition I have is incurable, so does that mean I'll be taking medication the rest of my life or will it require something worse?" Jeremiah watched his friend drop his eyes as though he were thinking of just the right words to say.

The sixty-year-old doctor knew he had studied every known report of the rare blood disorder his young friend had contracted. The outcome was always the same results: Rapid decline in the blood cells. No known cure. Fatal within weeks. Doctor Wells cleared his throat, stood up and made his way slowly around his desk then stopped in front of the young minister he had grown to love as a dear friend. He slowly placed his hand on Jeremiah's shoulder.

"Jeremy, you are such a fine young man and one heck of a preacher. It is obvious your members love their minister, my friend. I cannot recall when Messiah Methodist Church has had every-single pew filled on Sundays, like it is now. Why, the buzz is going around that the building committee are drawing up plans for a new-larger sanctuary." There was a sincere-brotherly love reflecting through Bennett Well's demeaner as he worked up his courage to say what needed to be said. "I know you have strong beliefs in God Jeremiah, unwavering faith. It is times like this thing you are facing, that requires a strong faith." The good doctor tried to smile before moving to the large window inside his office. He gazed down at the tranquil garden courtyard just under his office window, fighting the tears that threaten to fall from his sad eyes. "Son, how can you tell someone you love what they have to face?"

Now it was the good preacher trying to bring comfort to a dear friend. "You simply say those four dreadful words Ben. Those words frozen on your caring lips. Jeremiah, you are dying!" Saying the words out loud made it final when he saw his friend and doctor's face fall into his hands and weep. The young minister walked over and took around his friend, who had seen him grow up from a troubled youth. "Ben, we all will die someday. My time is just coming sooner than I had thought." Jeremiah kept strong through comforting others, even if their cause for weeping was over his final report. To help his friend, he would move forward with his questions.

"Ben, what could have brought on this rare blood disorder? It could not have been from an unhealthy life style. I always ate the right kind of food, ran every morning, even on rainy mornings. I worked out at the gym three-times a week and more important, I prayed many times throughout my day and read my bible regularly." Jeremiah waited for Doctor Wells to turn back around, his composure renewed.

"Jeremiah, this is a complicated condition that has only affected certain adults who have been abuse as a child." Bennett looked into the young minister's eyes. "Jeremy, I recall your birth father used to be known for drinking and carousing at the local pub every night. I have had men tell me he would grow loud and his drunken anger would result in arguments. Sometimes ending up in a brawl. This condition is all linked to severe trauma for childhood abuse, most time from one or more parent or some other trusted adult. The obnoxious crime could have been sexual or physical, such as sever hitting or slapping. The latter act would fit Harvey Mitchell's profile better." The doctor had been studying the pastor's face while he spoke and noticed a dark cloud pass over his usually gentle eyes. "Son, do you recall something like I described just now?"

3

Joan Byrd

"I had buried that horrible memory far back in my mind Ben, hoping it would not reservice, but in the end, that devil has a chance to repay me, death for death!" Jeremiah took a deep breath. "I had just turned ten-years-old and my dear mother had known how much I wanted my own ball and bat ever since every-other boy in the neighborhood had the pair. I don't know how she managed to scrape up enough money to buy them, since father couldn't hold a job due to his drinking habit. Poor mama did every available job that came her way. House cleaning, taking in laundry, baking, cooking and help watch other people's children. The gentle woman worked her fingers to the bone but never got any praise from the old man. The only demanding words he could give her was give me my share of that money woman!" tears came to Jeremiah's eyes. "He made sure he got his 1/3rd to waste buying whiskey and prostitutes down at the pub." His eyes fell on his friend, patiently listening. "I hated that old man and no matter how hard I tried to follow the holy book about loving my enemy and praying for them, this was one man I could never love and the only prayers I could pray for, was to asked my loving God to make something happen to the rotten devil!"

"Jeremy, I know it is hard to respect someone who acts the way your father acted toward your mother. Acting like he had the right to take money she had worked so hard for, then spend it like he had earned it, on cheap woman and booze." Bennett Wells knew there had to be more, so he needed to hear his young friend say why he really hated his father so much he wanted him dead. "Taking money like he did surely isn't the real reason you wanted that man out of your life for good. I know you son. You can take a lot of nonsense before you began to show anger, so what triggered off the need to see him dead?"

"That night mama surprised me with not only my gift, the bat and baseball, she had made me my favorite cake for my birthday. The dear saint even managed to get candles and while she was singing happy birthday to me, things turned very ugly. Father returned early from the tavern, completely drunk as usual and grew angry when he saw my cake, covered with ten candles aglow. Then he shouted for me to blow out the stupid

4

candles before it set the place on fire. Mama then reminded the devil that I had earned a birthday this year since I had been helping her do our chores at home to free up more time for her to work. With his raving and yelling, we knew why he came home early. He needed more money before he could return to the pub. The irresponsible man had gambled away every penny given to him and had assumed mama spent what little extra was left on me for my birthday." Jeremiah walked to the window, knowing what he had to tell him next was hard to say, man to man. "Red-face from anger, my old man made his way to me and grabbed my ball and gave it a toss across the room, breaking one of mama's priceless vases, the last thing her own mother had given her when she got married. "Ben, it has been twenty-years and I can still see my mama's tears falling."

Twenty-Years: Earlier

"I CANNOT BELIEVE YOU WASTED MY MONEY ON THIS BOY OF YOURS, YOU WORTHLESS HAG!" Harvey Mitchell yelled loudly.

Jeremiah had taken enough. He could not stand quiet and let that drunk devil call his mother names and he certainly would defend her from any more beatings. "LISTEN, YOU, DRUNK, NO-COUNT JERK, DON'T YOU EVER CALL MY BEAUTIFUL MOTHER AN UGLY NAME AGAIN! THE MONEY SHE MAKES IS NOT YOURS, YET SHE GIVES YOU 1/3RD OF IT TO WASTE OR THROW AWAY! NOW, YOU'VE MADE HER CRY BY BREAKING THE VASE HER MAMA GAVE HER WHEN SHE MARRIED YOUR SORRY ASS!" the young ten-year-old knew that he had taken his evil father off guard speaking back to him so bravely, but he was aware his spell would soon break and the bad man would be twice as mean.

"Why you little brat!" Without hesitation, the anger man slung his hand across the boy's face, causing him to hit the floor with a thug. Before he could wave his helpless mother away, she had made a wild dash over to protect her baby.

"Get your lousy hand's off Jeremiah and GET OUT!"

Harvey grabbed her by the shoulders and started shaking

her out of control. "YOU HAVE THE NERVE TO TELL ME TO GET OUT, BITCH!" His eyes burned down on her. "WE SHALL SEE WHO LEAVES MY HOUSE! IN A ZIP-LOCK BAG!"

"NO! LET MY MAMA GO, YOU BASTARD, OR I'LL KILL YOU!" Jeremiah cried out, fear racing through his body as he pulled at his large father who only laughed at him and knocked him back.

"Just stay out of my way boy or you will go with her." The evil man gave his wife an evil smile. "Then with the both of you gone, I can bring my broads back here instead of that cheap motel."

"Harvey, you know you can't get a job." Clara tried to reason with her angry husband by hitting him where she knew it would really hurt. No more free money to have his fun with. "I spoke out of defense for our son, for hurting him. You're not such a bad man when you're sober. You know I will continue to work to keep up our bills and give you spending money. But, if I'm gone, and you cannot find work, then the rent can't be paid and you'll be kicked to the streets to beg. Is that what you want. Those whores won't feel pity for you. Wouldn't you rather me stay alive to support the man I married for better or worse?"

"Will you promise not to buy the boy any more useless gifts or waste money on a cake for him." Harvey calmed down as he glanced over to find the young boy eyeing him with caution. "What's with that look boy? Don't you trust me to except your mother's peace offering?"

"I would sir if I for one-minute thought you were being truthful." Jeremiah was taught to always tell the truth. "If I knew you were being honest with mother, I would quickly agree I should never receive another gift or cake if it meant keeping the peace in our home. I might even grow to respect you just a little bit. Start coming to church with us on Sundays and I can guarantee you will have my full respect sir."

"What have we here Clara, a little preacher?" Harvey belted out a loud laugh. "Keep your useless respect boy as well as that so call religion! I had rather gather with the heathen, as you church goers call us normal people having fun and living the good life!" His cold stare fell on his wife. "See what you have raise Clara? A no-a-count, holy freak!" the obnoxious drunk weaved his way over to the serious face boy and picked up a water pitcher and smiling, dumped the entire gallon over Jeremiah's head. "I baptize you, idiot of the week!" he got down to get in his face, the smell of alcohol reeking on his breath. "Ask me to church, will you? I'll just fix your wagon boy!"

Harvey Mitchell tried to stand up straight and almost tossed over before catching himself laughing, then made his way back to his nervous wife. "Look Clara, I shall take you up on your kind offer if you do one thing for me?"

The worried mother glanced at her young son before responding. "What else can I do for you Harvey? I already give you a third of my earnings. It takes the rest for bills and food, all come non-stop."

"Oh, I would never ask you for more than my share Clara. My request must be fulfilled or this bargain is off!" He glanced back at his son, standing rigid, afraid to hear what he was asking for. "I want you to stop taking that boy and yourself to that worthless church service from now on! I insist that you remove that old bible you read to him every night and take down the two pictures of this man you worship! I never want to hear his name spoken in this house again! Just tell me you will disown him and things will be peaceful with me."

Mother and son could only look at one another, knowing the full impact of what would happen the moment they refused to give in to this evil man's declaration. All peaceful bets would be off the table and someone would lose more than just their life. Jeremiah stood straight, knowing his words might get him killed by this man who had fathered him, but he was a Christian, a lamb of the Lord and he would never disown Jesus.

"Sir, I will speak for myself! I fear it is the devil inside you that makes you say these things against your Holy Creator, and even though my life may be cut short by an aggressive father, who hates the very sight of me and my precious mother, I can never disown the One who died such a painful life on that cross for my sins! FOR ALL OUR SINS FATHER! Yours included! But this free gift will do you no good unless you change, not us, not mama or me. We will live on in heaven where love abounds and all is happy with Jesus forever! I will never be ashamed to say, I am a Christian and my heart, soul, and life belongs to my Savior, Jesus Christ!"

"Our son is right Harvey. Jeremiah and I are redeemed by the blood of the Lamb! Neither one of us are ready to die yet, for only God can call us home when our time on earth is finished, but Jeremiah and I are both ready. We will know Jesus the moment He appears to us, by the nail prints in His hands and feet." Clara stood like a soldier of the cross, knowing she probably would be killed by the man she married. Knowing there might not be any witness if he killed them both, the wise mother had removed the phone receiver while her wild husband had been harassing Jeremiah and dialed 911 and laid it out of sight. "I cannot do as you ask Harvey! I will attend Church with my son as long as I have breath, and I will read His Holy word until I close my eyes to see Him face to face. Jesus Christ is my Lord and Savior, the Almighty Father and the Holy Spirit make them the Holy Trinity-three-in-one! Our Eternal life will be in heaven, but Harvey, unless you have an awakening, you will spend your eternity in Hell, with Lucifer."

"ENOUGH OF YOUR PREACHING! I WARNED YOU!" The irate man yelled.

"And we warned you father! If we all die today we will go to a far better place than you will! To burn for all eternity will be your fate and I pray to God it wasn't so. I would not wish that punishment on my worse enemy." Jeremiah was only ten, but he knew his calling was to be a minister when he grew up, but now he feared his life might be cut short by his own father. "Sir, you are my birth father and my faith has taught me to love you, but I cannot like the mistreatment you give to your devoted wife, my saintly mother nor the constant beatings you deliver to me every single day!" Jeremiah squeezed the bat handle after glancing at his mother, trembling from deadly fear. "This abuse stops today father! One way or the other! Make your decision count!"

"You think you're pretty smart don't you kid? You use such clever words, trying to get inside my head, but you see, those big empty words do you no good!" The drunken man gave a menacing grin. "Do you want to hit me over the head with that cheap bat boy? Have you grown into the protector of your weak mother? Do you have what it takes to TAKE DOWN A RAGING BULL?"

"Perhaps, not by myself, but with the shield of my powerful Lord I can take down the meanest giant standing in my way! Just like King David when he was about my age!" Jeremiah held his ground, his fate strong with unwavering faith.

An evil laugh escaped Harvey Mitchell's mouth. "You, stupid boy! Believe in fairy tale books, do you? I will wrap that cheap bat around your puny neck, you, useless kid!" The angry man headed for Jeremiah while Clara picked up the broken vase and raced behind him, aiming for his big head. After smashing it over his head, cutting a large gash across his sneering face, he slung around and knocked her across the floor where she slammed into the wall, breaking her neck.

Jeremiah stared in shocked horror, knowing from the loud cracking sound his mama was dead. He turned to see his father swaying from the hard hit, but he quickly straightened up, his dark eyes directly toward his frighten son. It was at that very moment the young boy heard the still-small voice of God speaking, just to him.

"Jeremiah, my son, be not afraid to fight this evil man, whose seed made a great messenger in you. Harvey Mitchell has been given chance after chance to be saved but has always made a mockery about His God. This night, Harvey will come face to face with my old enemy, then he shall believe the words you and your pure mother spoke but now too late for his eternity. The misfortunate man will keep staring into your eyes child, trying to break you down and make you weak. He does Lucifer's bidding, but unbeknown to him or Lucifer, your guardian angel will aid you in this battle, same as the young David's did many-years-ago, in earth years. When Harvey charges, thinking to kill you, you will be waiting. You will feel the bat, now strong as steel in the grip of Devin, your appointed guardian. It will rise for battle and strike the foe in the temple. In his drunken state he will wonder backward, toward the window, now open by the dark angel waiting below, who thinks it's your screaming body that will be tossed down in his waiting arms. Beware, the enemy advances!"

Like a charging bull, the lost man with hate-filled eyes rushed toward his son, standing tall, holding the bat steady, still down by his side. When Harvey Mitchell got in striking distanced, arms out ready to take-out his son's life, the bat swung up high and came down hard, against the side of the dangerous man's head, sending him reeling backward in awkward movements until he reached the open window. Trying to catch himself in his drunken daze, for a brief moment he witnessed who waited below and in a stricken panic called out for his son.

"Help me son!" he felt himself slipping. "Please Jeremiah, save me!" unable to hold on, the abusive father, who had murdered his loving wife in front of his ten-year-old son, slipped to his own death and was swept away by Satan.

CHAPTER 2

Doctor Bennett Well's Office

Jeremiah felt his old friend's hand on his back and turned to face him after reliving the nightmare with him. "The police showed up too late for my precious mama but they knew everything that happened from the 911 operator, who had listened in horror after contacting the police. They apologized for not getting here in time to save my parents from my father's drunken spree. They had to trace down the phone call then find our house. I was considered not guilty for my father's death since he was driven to kill me."

"Where did they take you Jeremy? You couldn't remain in that house alone, not at ten, or after everything that happened there." Doctor Wells led the weak man to a chair.

"I had been so upset over my mama's death and the fact that I felt somewhat responsible for possibly making matters worse and it ended up with her coming to my defense." The young minister felt fresh tears welling in his eyes. "I kept thinking, mama stay where you are, I can fight my father and win, like David did. But, I could not tell her or make any jesters to make her understand I had a plan to rid ourselves of this dangerous drunk forever." Jeremiah dropped his head. "I hadn't even considered what would happen to me after both my parents were gone. It was only until deputy Carter mentioned the state orphanage that I realize I was now an orphan. I had been staying by myself before when mama was working and father was out boozing or out cold at one of his cheap model rooms. I just assumed I could continue staying home, but sheriff Shaffer had to go by the book, as he called it. A kid my age with no parents to keep him up, had no other alternative. So, I was sent to the state orphanage and ran away the next day. I remembered the outside vents at Messiah Methodist Church were surrounded by a neatly trimmed boxwood bush, to hide the steam vents coming out." Jeremiah glanced up smiling,

Joan Byrd

remembering happier days. "I had recalled hiding in there when my friends and I were playing hide and seek and they finally had to give up searching, so I slipped out without them seeing me and told them I was hiding in plain sight right behind them. They all laughed and declared me the winning fibber, and insisted I reveal my hiding place. I declined, hoping to fool them again but they changed games on me." The sad events had made the young man weary. "Well, after running from the orphanage, that made me feel like a prisoner after all the talk about me not being guilty for my father's death, I finally made it back to the Outer Banks unseen. I made my home inside the boxwoods and wrapped up in my blankets I retrieved from our locked down house. I also took things I could use and made frequent trips there whenever I needed something. The vents were run from both the heat furnace and the air condition unit, so whatever the weather outside, I remained comfortable. I would help myself to food, fruit, water and other items like books in the church's outside pantry for the needy, and I was in need. A tarp kept me dry when it rained or snowed, so my life-style turned into camping. I called it home for four months and everything changed the day Reverend Russell found me huddled under my makeshift tent during a thunderstorm."

Messiah Methodist Church: Twenty-Years Ago

There had been a board meeting that evening and everyone finished their reports by seven, so the tired group filed out, dashing to their cars as the first drops of rain started belting down. I heard two men shutting the church doors and locking them before the one with his back to me made the statement: 'I thought the meeting went well tonight George. It looks like we're in for a bad storm tonight. Have you heard anything about that Mitchell boy? It seems a shame the kid is lost somewhere out there, fighting the elements.'" I listened as Mr. Russell spoke with concern in his strong voice.

"Andy, that young man has been missing for four months as of today. I cannot begin to imagine how I would feel over losing both parents in such a tragic way." His umbrella popped up as he prepared for his own mad dash to his automobile

12

waiting nearby. "That boy is strong-willed and capable of eluding those searching for him. It breaks my heart to think Jeremy feels like he cannot trust anyone. Andy, I would take that dear boy in this second if it were possible."

"You are a man of God George and I know first-hand that you are a firm believer in prayer." Andy Johnson pulled his raincoat hood over his head at the first sound of distant thunder. "Why not asked God to guide the runaway boy back to Messiah Methodist Church, the one place he had always felt safe and full of Christian love. If God answers that prayer, then you can help the lad." Andy jumped at the clap of thunder getting closer. "Better make that prayer for tomorrow George. I wouldn't want anyone to get caught out this stinker! I'm sure Jeremy has found shelter!" He glanced out and waved as he dashed to his truck. "Take care preacher and don't worry none about that kid! He's as smart as they come!" With that 'not so great' advice, the fifty-five-year-old dock worker jumped behind the wheel of his '72 ford pickup and drove away.

"Don't worry? That's easy for you to say, Andy Johnson with a house filled with six sons still living at home with their families!" The preacher mumbled as he locked the doors. "I bet old calm Andy would grow concern if it was one of his kids lost somewhere out there in the dark-stormy-night." Reverend Russell looked up into the stormy clouds, barely visible now that darkness was fast approaching and said a heartfelt prayer for Jeremiah Mitchell. Then a strange, yet miraculous sign from God appeared in the stormy sky. A lightning bolt streaked straight down while a second lightning bolt crossed it, revealing a lighted cross in the night sky. Tears streamed down the minister's face, knowing it was an answer to his prayer, but what did it mean?

"Tell me Lord, does this heavenly sign show me the boy is now in heaven with you?" no longer worried about the storm or the fact he was getting wet by the downpour, George Russell dropped to his knees. "Speak to your humble servant Lord and tell me if the boy is still alive that my wife and I might take him as our own. To raise in a godly manner, give him everything a son requires to live a happy life. Make sure he gets the best

13

possible education to be whatever you want him to be." His head dropped, as he listened for the voice of God. In the noise of the deep thunder, the devoted servant of God heard a soft whisper near his ear.

"My brother, thou art full of love and compassion for the young boy. He is not yet with me but rest in the tall-green hedge-wall, very near to you. Young Jeremiah feels safe and at home near the place he learned of me with his beloved mother Clara." The voice began to fade. "Go to him and receive him into thine home and heart, my faithful servant."

Doctor Well's Office: Twenty-Years-Later

"He found me there, fast asleep, yet trembling from the loud crashes of thunder." Jeremiah remember the loving couple that took him in and adopted him. "They treated me as their own and I finally knew what it felt like to have a father that loved me completely, as I did him. Nancy was so much like my own dear mama, it was easy to love her and address her as my mama. I graduated with honors and a degree from Duke Divinity school. The Lord blessed me with the gift of powerful sermons that were guaranteed to put me in a large church right out of college but as you must know, I chose one of the smalless churches in the state of North Carolina." He gave a weak smile. "I could never turn down all those beautiful Christians who had become my church family since I walked in those doors with my saintly mama." He glanced up at his friend, eyes wet with fresh tears. "Now I must leave them and I cannot bring myself to tell them I am leaving and why?" Jeremiah stood up and paced the floor. "Should I tell my brethren what happened the night my parents died?" he could hear the officer telling him his mother was dead: 'I'm sorry son, your mother is dead! Her neck has been broken!' "Father had killed my mama! I killed my father! It was my fault! If I hadn't wanted that stupid bat and ball, my mama would not have died! I slammed that bat against his head and stood frozen, watching as he kept falling back, toward that window!"

"Jeremy, it was in self-defense for yourself and your mother when you hit your intoxicated father." The gentle friend gathered his hand in his own. "You said the Lord spoke to you saying: 'Be not afraid to fight this man.' He also said Devin, your angel would help you in the battle. Son, the one thing every Tri-Lexica patient have in common is their anxiety for feeling some personal guilt from their actions that brought on the beatings and in cases like yours, the act of murder." The caring doctor watched his friend closely and could see raw emotions sweep across his handsome features. "Jeremy, could this be the reason your advance aggression of this fatal disease has evolved so rapidly?'

"The gilt always hit in the dead of night when I have reoccurring nightmares about that night." Jeremiah spoke as though he were in a foggy trance. "It all plays out in my mind exactly as it happened and ends exactly like I recall. The dream now is so familiar that I can slow down the part where the soft words are and I have a hard time determining just who is really speaking to me!" the preacher got eye contact with his friend. "Do not think I have lost my faith in the Almighty God Ben, from my questioning the one speaking to me in a calm-sure voice. Yes, it is true the Lord would be aware of his dark angel being near but I cannot forget how the loving voice almost sounded mocking when he mentioned his enemy was waiting below the window."

"Jeremy, are you saying, you believe the one speaking was not the Lord Jesus, but indeed the deceitful enemy himself, edging you on so he could collect this one's soul before you or your mother caused his victim to repent and be saved?" Bennett could see how the devil could pretend to be the Lord to achieve his evil goal.

"That is exactly what I feel has happened. As I stood there frozen in fear, I could hear words fill my head from my Sunday-school teacher, our preacher, George Russell, who took me in. Words that contradicted the voice I heard." Nervous with anxious anxiety, Jeremiah jumped up and moved again to the window. "Words written in the Holy Book! Words to guide our actions! THOU SHALT NOT KILL! LOVE THY ENEMY AND PRAY FOR THEM! DO UNTO OTHERS AS YOU WOULD HAVE OTHERS DO UNTO YOU! IF SOMEONE

STRIKES YOUR RIGHT CHEEK, TURN THE OTHER CHEEK!" Tears of remorse fell from his eyes. "Then the repeating words that haunted me the most commanded my thoughts. HELP SAVE THE LOST, ER THEY SHOULD PERISH INTO EVERLASTING HELL!" Jeremiah turned, weeping uncontrollable tears. "Ben, my father begged me to help him! His last words to me were: 'Please, Jeremiah, save me!' Don't you see, if my father had not died in sin, then maybe there would have been some slim chance to save him. If not as the ten-year-old boy he saw before going into eternal suffering but the man I have become." He shook his head sadly. "Now, it's too late to save him! My chances have gone and Lucifer has claimed his immortal soul for himself. I fear it is my father's wicked spirit that has drove me to this fatal disease that is robbing my body of life. Or maybe it is my punishment from God for believing the deceiver instead of waiting for His saving grace when my father finally saw his fate after he glanced down and saw pure evil looking up, waiting for him to let go. I should have broke free from the demon's grip and rush forward to pulled my father back!"

"Jeremy, you must not keep blaming yourself and you must not think our loving Lord in heaven blames you for that wicked man's choices, nor his unfortunate death." Bennett Wells reached around his young friend in a fatherly hug. "You cannot keep beating yourself up over something that could never have had a happy ending. Yes, there might have been a slight chance that your father would have been grateful for saving him, had you rush forward to pull him back to safety. But, the chances were far greater that he would have taken you down with him, out of spite."

"The sad truth is, I will never know." Jeremy collected his emotions and gave his old friend a weak smile. "Now that my time is cut short, there is one thing I have always wanted to do before I left this earth. So, before it's too late to fulfill my one wish, I must turn in my resignation at Messiah Methodist." He reached over to pat his friend on the back. "I'm going to miss our fishing trips out on the Atlantic, now that you finally taught me how to reel in something besides someone's missing flipflop or swim trunks. Think about me sometimes when you reel in an old thermos bottle, alright buddy?"

"Now, don't start saying goodbye yet Jeremy." The sentimental doctor felt a lump invade his throat over the young minister's words. "There's always hope this diagnosis might be wrong, but even if it is Tri-Lexica decease, you may overcome it. Stop thinking of the worse and keep a positive outlook. We human doctors can only do so much Jeremy, then comes God! Let's pray for that miracle only He can give."

CHAPTER 3

Back on the Sunset Beach

"You are a good man Bennett Wells." Jeremiah spoke against the strong sea breeze. "Maybe the Lord's reenactment will give me that miracle you spoke of dear friend." He thought back to the conversation on the phone with the Christian Tours director just before coming down on the beach. "I have already received one miracle. First, the tour to the Holy Land were totally booked for the Easter reenactment and all spots taken to carry the cross a short distance had been filled. I was told I would have to wait for next year's Easter tour." Jeremiah gave a sarcastic chuckle. "Next Easter! My lifeless body will be cold in the grave on Easter morning and the graveyard admirers will walk over my grave and shed a tear while they admire the arrangement of flowers placed there by my grieving stepparents, George and Nancy Russell." Jeremy felt fresh tears returning but they were not for his promised passing, but for the two-beautiful people who took him in and raised him as their own.

"Dear Nan and George, I must tell them I won't be here to share our twenty-first year as a family this May." He looked out at the vast ocean and could remember all their family days together on this very spot. His heart ached for them for the young man had never loved anyone but his mother more. "Who will be there to place flowers on their grave when I am gone? I cannot leave such loving people without someone to keep their grave adorned with flowers, especially on Easter. I have some money set aside that I won't be needing anymore, so I will set up a trust at Marsh Cove Nursery and have them choose a perfect vase of the Lemon-Lavender Lilac arrangement each Easter. A combination of both their favorite flowers."

Jeremiah didn't see the small woman searching for seashells behind him and how she listened to his words as he spoke out, thinking he was alone on the beach. Unable to remain quiet a moment longer, she broke the silence, the need to speak to this sad young man.

"Please forgive me for listening to your one-sided conversation young man." The petite grey hair lady gave him a cheery smile when he turned quickly around, feeling embarrassed for being caught talking to himself. Jeremiah glanced down at the bucket in her hand, filled with a collection of small seashells. "I heard you mention Dan and George. Such a lovely-God-fearing couple. They have lived here at the Cove for as long as I have." The spry little lady stepped back to size the young man up. "Oh my, do not tell me you are that ten-year-old boy they took in some twenty-years-ago!"

"Why, yes ma'am, I am he. Jeremiah Mitchell Russell. I go by Reverend Mitchell now so folks won't be getting me and dad mixed up." He couldn't help but to smile at such an active little lady with obvious pep. "Do you know my stepparents very well?"

"Oh, my yes I do! I have been observing their good deeds for years! That I have!" Her lop-sided smile started to grow on the young preacher and there was something about her charming manner that made him feel some better. "Why, even in their late sixties they saw a need to take in a lost child, see to his needs and care, then treat him as their own. Not many souls knew just how much Nan and George desired to have a child of their own and you just filled that sad empty place in their heart like magic."

"Yes ma'am, they saved me from the streets." Jeremiah smiled as he recalled the stormy night Reverend Russell found him sound asleep outside the church. "I had managed to stay awake long enough to hear the first part of George and Andy's conversation concerning me and my whereabouts. I recall smiling to myself, knowing how close I was to them as they spoke, then I heard a clap of thunder followed by Andy's nervous voice, urging the minister to go home, then wait and pray in the morning and not to worry about the boy. The thunder grew louder and muffled out the voices so I fell asleep listening to the rain and thunder on my tarp roof. I heard someone call my name and I was shocked to find George

19

standing over me looking down with loving eyes, wet with grateful tears." Jeremiah couldn't hold back his new tears at the thought of leaving these two-beautiful people. "Then he took me inside the church and gave me something warm to eat and patiently listen as I begged him not to take me back to that horrible orphanage. My dear lady, I can still hear his words to me. The words that changed my life and turn me around. Reverend Russell led me to the church chapel and we sat down facing one-another, then he spoke."

"Jeremiah, I would never send you back to that orphanage when there is a loving-caring couple who would love to adopt you, if the courts approve it. My beloved Nan, Nancy to most people except close friends, and I would feel blessed to have you become our own son, if you will permit two people, already well into their 60's to be your adopted parents."

"I could not think of a better set for my stepmother and stepfather and I tearfully agreed. Nan and George did adopt me and gave me a loving home with no abuse." The thoughts of leaving them swept through his mind like a mournful song, leaving him down trodden. "Mama Nan and George, my dad, loves me like their own son and I know them well. They will miss their boy until their own dying day."

"And that is why you want to make sure their graves, once laid in by their final earthy journey, have the flowers they loved, placed there from you, since you will no longer be there in person to do it yourself." The elderly lady shook her head sadly before reaching for another perfect pink shell and placing it in the overflowing bucket.

Jeremiah felt the need to change the subject, so he asked the obvious question. "Dear lady, what do you do with all those beautiful-colorful shells?"

She responded with her lop-sided smile. "I make lovely jewelry out of them. Let me show you." She lit up with excitement as she pulled up an extremely attractive necklace from around her tan neck and held it out for him to admire. He gazed down in amazement at the perfect strand of pink shells, connecting so close that joined as one link and dangling on the end was a brilliant cross made from white sea sticks glued together. The rising moon shone down on the cross and it came to life with glittering sparkles of light. "I make things like this heaven's light holy cross necklace. Jewelry featuring heaven's angels as well as the sacred cross. Rings, earrings, bracelets as well as necklaces! I sale my things at Miss Fannie's Gift Shop, just up the beach a way. I have been selling my shell jewelry at that shop for as long as I remember and she sales a lot of my things to the tourist coming through Marsh Cove."

"That cross you are wearing is truly stunning. I've never seen another one like it." Jeremiah smiled down at her happy face. "Is this how you make your income, doing this thing you obviously love to be out here so late, gathering shells?"

"Heaven no young man, I do not need an extra income. This is my service work for my Lord. We all do loving service for the Holy-Three-in-One!" another lop-sided smile was given. "I happen to know you do a great service for the Almighty as well." She announced brightly. "I collect my weeks earnings and send them straight to St, Jude Hospital for Children. You know, to help all those precious little souls that are suffering. Why, after what my Savior went and done for me, that is the lease I can do in His name."

"My dear lady, that is a great service for our Lord, a true loving servant helping those in need. It is a pity there aren't more God-fearing people like you." Jeremiah felt at peace talking to this precious woman with the lop-sided smile. "Can I ask you what your name is?"

"Most certainly Jeremiah, since I already know your name and who it was that took you in to raise after your own dear mother left for heaven. You can rest assured your mama is safe from any more abuse living among the angels and our Lord." He considered how this stranger knew so much about his mother's death, but had assumed being friends with Nan and George, she was told what happened. "My name is Fran Tatum and I live up the beach away. Nan and George said you had become a great minister of the word."

"Somehow, I felt the calling when I was 10-years-old and it just felt right to become a preacher like my dad, George. Since he retired, I took over as pastor for Messiah Methodist

Church, about two-miles up Marsh Cove Road." He looked out to see the moon rising higher over the water. "Do you attend Church anywhere on the Cove Fran?"

"My yes, every Sunday. I would not miss a single sermon given by that young preacher that shows up every-single-Sunday at Sunrise." Her eyes seemed to twinkle in the moonlight. "Sunrise is a perfect time for a beach service. Sitting there on my old lawn chair watching the first rays of sunlight rise up out of God's heavenly created ocean while the Holy man spins a biblical story that lights up the beach with glorious sunrise."

"So, this preacher just shows up every Sunday, to preach to the people living on the beach front?" Jeremiah had not heard of any services being led on the beach at Marsh Cove. The small community had four churches of different denominations and plenty of room for every citizen in Marsh Cove. "I have lived here for 30-years Fran and I have never heard about any beach worship services. May I ask what the preacher's name is?"

"I do not mind at all Jeremy, but unfortunately the religious man has never mention his name and done of us attending has ever asked him, until this past Sunday" She gave her perfect lop-sided smile. "Our small group of twelve arrive just before daybreak to arrange our chairs and just before the sun appears, the preacher is standing before us. His presence is like no other man I have heard speak and his voice draws you into all his little stories he shares." Fran gave a soft laugh. "And when he has finished telling us the story, it always has a beautiful meaning with a purpose behind it." Fran paused to think a moment. "He told us what he called all his stories, but for the life of me I cannot remember what it was. Old age I guess."

"Would they be called, Parables?" Jeremiah couldn't understand why he was having goose-bumps just listening to this sweet lady giving her description of this minister that just seems to appear in front of them from out of the blue. He waited while she shook her head, happy to recall the word. "Fran, can you describe what this young man looks like? If he is a fellow minister on the Cove then I might recognize him and give you a name."

"I am terribly afraid you could never guess who this preacher is from any of our local churches Jeremy." She reached up to pat his head. "You see, this Holy man has never gone to divinity school. He did not have too. The young man gets his knowledge from higher places. I believe, when asked which college he attended, he said that his degree was not of this world." She gave her signature smile. "Now, to describe the heavenly preacher. He stands a little taller than your 6ft 8", he's has a Jewish kind of look, with shoulder length hair that cascades in curls. His handsome face is a pleasure to look at, as is his loving smile. I have never seen a neater beard and mustache on another reverent man and his simply white robe always glistens as the sun arises." Fran could not resist her soft laughter over Jeremiah's dropped jaw. "I see you are thinking the exact same thing I do every time we are bless to hear him preach." She glanced up as if to question the young man in front of her. "You are thinking Jesus, right?" Fran could tell the young man was speechless, so she continued. "I had been thinking that for some time Jeremy, so last Sunday morning before he left, I just came out and asked him if he was my Lord, Jesus."

"What did he say to you Fran?" Jeremiah finally felt like he could breathe normal.

"He just looked down into my eyes with those heavenly blue-green eyes and smiled, then whispered before disappearing, I am called Jesu."

"Jesu, Jesus!" Jeremiah felt his body weaving and Fran reached over and held him up to steady him.

"Jeremiah, you have nothing to fear. Jesus will go before you into the Holy City of Jerusalem. You will be granted your wish to carry the sacred cross the last track to Calvary, then wait near the cross as it is risen up. The cross you carry will go up holding a reenactor, tied to the cross to make it appear real. Then, what you will see cannot be seen by any other person watching. The image of the lamb of God will become visible for your eyes only to witness Jesus's death on the cross." Fran's voice had taken on a younger voice as she continued. "Listen closely and do as I tell you if you wish to be made whole by the blood of Jesus. When you witness the sacred blood of Jesus flowing down the cross, move up close to the cross. Let no man stop you as you reach up and touch the Holy blood of the Lamb, then spread the blood on your forehead and you shall be REDEEMED BY THE BLOOD OF THE LAMB!"

Jeremiah felt his tears blurring his vision as he tried to make out the shell lady who was removing the cross from around her neck. "Jeremiah, lower you head so I can place this sacred cross around your head." Fran lovingly lifted the glowing cross over his dark hair and he suddenly felt at peace with what he was facing. "Wear this sacred cross throughout your life Jeremiah and the Lord will be with you always. Follow what I told you and at the cross you will be saved from this disease that seeks to rob your life. Your God has greater plans for you son, so be at peace. You will find your request to leave for Israel has been arranged and your spot in the reenactment has been placed." With that, Fran and her overflowing basket of colorful shells had vanished, leaving Jeremiah searching for her footprints he had seen only moments before, now gone.

CHAPTER 4

Jeremiah stood, pondering what had just happened on the moonlit beach and for a brief moment he considered the fact that it was the turmoil he was facing that made his mind react irrational. The face of the petite lady wearing a lop-sided grin, came into his mind and he slowly pondered her words. How could that sweet stranger, make her way so quickly inside his heart and her manner and faith-filled words bring him such joy and incredible peace to his troubled soul.

The ocean breeze swept around him, gently blowing the sacred cross against his heart causing his eyes to drop to see it there, right where the shell-lady had placed it, while speaking a message from God in a young woman's voice, instead of the shaky voice Fran had used.

"Dear Fran, are you really an angel, disguised as an older woman who collects shells for making jewelry?" his fingers touched the exquisite necklace around his neck and instantly a white dove flew down and brushed his cheek before rising above the clouds. He followed the heavenly dove out of sight as he whispered, now alone on the dark beach. "It wasn't my imagination or wishful thinking. Fran was as real as that moonlit ocean and the tranquil peaceful hope I felt listening to her speak was really the voice of God's messenger showing me the way."

True to the shell-lady's words, an overnight package from The Christian tours, was waiting for Jeremiah by his door. The package held two passes. The ticket for one-full-week in Jerusalem and the card he had prayed for, the last cross barer, from the last third mile through the narrow streets and up the steep hill that leads to Golgotha where he will see the place the Savior of the world died.

Jeremiah had only a couple of weeks left before he left the North Carolina coast for Israel, so the need to find the gift shop the elderly lady told him about was high on his list. Fran Tatum had seemed so convincing, the young minister just had to go check it out for himself. It didn't take him long to find Fannie's Gift Shop since it appeared to be the oldest building on the beachfront.

Jeremiah walked in and the sound of a bell rang out over the door and he chuckled softly from hearing the old timey sound. The instant he looked around he felt he had stepped back in time and there appeared to be no one attending the front checkout. Once again, an old fashion bell caught his eye, so he walked over to give it a slap, then grinned at the loud dinging sound. Hearing footsteps on the old pine floors above his head he looked up to see a beautiful young lady looking down.

"I thought I heard the bell ring over the door!" Struck by her perfect features, Jeremiah enjoyed her friendly smile. "Welcome to Fannie's Gift Shop! I'll be right down." He watched her move and followed her shapely legs as she hurried down an old staircase. "I was just straightening up the antique balcony. It's usually not busy this time of morning and it gives me time to clean-up after the antique seekers, who don't mind diving in a stack of old things." She brushed away a falling curl, when she finally noticed how handsome her customer was. "You are new to the shop, Mister?"

"It's Reverend Mitchell, madam and you are Miss or Mrs.?" he smiled.

"It is Reverend Stevens sir, Cassondra Stevens." She knew she had taken him off guard. "I just finished Duke Divinity University and I'm currently waiting for a church to become available." Cassie gave him a genuine smile. "Tell me Reverend Mitchell, where do you preach? Maybe I'll drop in one Sunday to hear what you preach about."

"Messiah Methodist would love to have you pay us a visit, Miss Stevens." Jeremiah finally took note they were the only two people in the shop. "Please call me Jeremiah, if you like, since we are fellow servants of the Lord."

"I would like that Jeremiah and you can call me Cassie." She knew she had been staring at the handsome clergyman so she quickly looked around. "Are you looking for anything in particular you wish to see?" she waved her hand around the rows of beach gifts.

"There is something I would very much like to see Cassie."
He glanced around the small, two-floor shop. "I was spending
some alone time last night on the beach and I'm embarrassed
to say, I had been talking my personal troubles a loud to myself,
never knowing I was being observed by one of the most
interesting elderly lady I've ever known. The 4ft. 7" lady
interrupted me to give me some really good advice over my
situation. I noticed the active senior was collecting seashells
and knew by her full bucket she had been at it for some time."
Jeremy saw he had the lovely young preacher fully drawn in to
what he was telling her so he continued. "I asked her what she
did with all those pretty colorful shells and she informed me
that she made necklaces and other pieces of jewelry with them
and sold them at Fannie's gift shop. The dear soul claims she
sales out before she can make another batch."

"Well, alright, that should be easy enough to look up for
you." Cassie walked behind the old counter and pulled out a
book ledger. "We have many talented shell artist, who sale their
finished products here. What is her name so I can look it up."

"Fran Tatum. I am certain you should know her. That little
lady can keep a soul entertain when she spends her life story."
Jeremiah noticed how quiet Cassie had gotten so glanced over
to find her staring at him seriously. "You do know Fran, surely
she stands out from all the other local artist. She said she had
lived here in Marsh Cove all her life. She knew my stepparents
very well and apparently everything there is to know about me,
as well."

"Reverend Michell, unless there is another shell artist who
makes jewelry named Fran Tatum, you must have been
scammed or misunderstood her name." The pretty salesclerk
closed the leger and pulled out one from underneath the
counter. She reached for a white cloth and dusted off the years
of neglect while the interested minister watched on.

"Look Miss Stevens, I know what I heard and saw and that
precious lady was anything but fake! I can prove Fran Tatum
makes beautiful seashell jewelry. Maybe you don't know her
because you're new to the Cove."

"I assure you 'Mr.' Mitchell that even if the precious lady

hasn't graced this old shop since I was hired, her name would have been inside that first ledger." She pushed the old book aside and pulled the new one back to look up Fran Tatum and found no such name in the ledger. "She is not mentioned in the latest ledger and if she sold out as she claimed, her totals would make up several pages, listing each item sold and the amount received."

"Try the older book, maybe she is in there since she has been selling here for years." Jeremy was getting anxious over finding the woman who seemed to turned into an angel. He just knew the shell-sacred cross necklace was real and she had claimed to make it."

"Listen Jeremiah, I know for a fact this dear lady you met last night could not be inside that old book."

Before he could interrupt her, Cassie held up her hand and turned the book around to face him and opened it to the last page. His eyes fell on the last entry marked: June 12, 1870 then back up into her eyes.

"Alright, you do not have a record of Fran Tatum, so please explain this beautiful gift she placed around my neck last night." Jeremiah gently pulled the pink shell necklace out and revealed the white cross dangling on the end. "Fran called it the" before Jeremy could get the name out, Cassie spoke the name, her eyes wide with shock.

"The Sacred Cross!" Cassie's shock turned to complete wonder, filled with extraordinary astonishment. "I know it shouldn't be the real thing, but after studying the Sacred Cross ever since I was old enough to help my dad in the Family's Antique Shop, I can see everything there that made this 1748 masterpiece the real deal!"

"Excuse me, did you say, 1748?" he watched her nod a positive, too caught up with the sheer reality that she was seeing something that had not been seen in well over 200-years. "Cassie, do you have anything in this old shop belonging to Fran?"

Cassie snapped back, reclaimed her emotions and looked up. "The shop has kept everything they could find belonging to Fran Tatum, due to her amazing talent. Being a good Christian woman, it was said Fran gave all the money she made away to the children's orphanage in the big city. I guess they were referring to Raleigh." She pointed to the loft. "Her display is in the Antique section, so please follow me and I will show you the last painting done of the lovely lady." Cassie clutched the old stair rail then glanced back. "Watch your step Jeremiah, these old steps go back to the 1700's."

"I knew this building was old Cassie, but how did it survive all those years this close to the ocean?" Jeremy stayed close behind the beautiful young woman and wondered why he was having butterfly feelings when she looked into his eyes.

"I have been told, this once fabulous building set far from the coastline. In the 1700's the ocean set farther away and no one built close to the beach back then, due to storms that swept in from across the vast water." She smiled as she stepped off the old staircase onto the wide pine plank floor. "Over the years the ocean crept closer inward and this is how it sits here today."

After reaching the top, his eyes fell on the painted portrait of the woman he had spoke with the previous night. His fast footsteps took him quickly to her display and he stared up at the shell-lady. "That's her Cassie! That is definitely Fran Tatum, the shell-lady!"

"Then she had to be a ghost. This was Fran's last picture before her death in 1760 and the dress she is wearing was the one recorded as her death dress."

Jeremiah got a closer look and noticed the Fran in the painting was wearing the Sacred Cross necklace. "Cassie, this is surreal! Not only was the Fran I was conversing with wearing the Sacred Cross, like she does in her picture, but, even though the sky had grown dim from twilight, I could see my companion was wearing that very same dress!"

"Then, she had to be a ghost, what other explanation could there be?" Cassie stated her case. "The same dress she was buried in and all reports state, the prize artist was buried wearing the cross that is now hanging around your neck!"

CHAPTER 5

The bell rang over the door below, and the couple broke their eye contact as Cassie scrambled over to the rail and looked down to see one of her regular customers. "Good morning Mrs. Templeton. If you are here for the Blue-Royal Ring replica, I am afraid I haven't been able to get in touch with Sir Frank Francis yet. It appears the renown jewelry artist has left the country for some sort of family matter."

"Oh, dear me, I was in hopes of having that exquisite ring made for my daughter, Helena's wedding next month." The woman called up destressed. "Whatever will I do if I cannot get that delightful Sir Francis to agree to make it on time? My daughter just insisted on having the Blue Royal ring, and of course she knows that she must settle for a replica of the Fran Tatum's most beautiful ring ever made! I mean, finding a perfect blue pearl from the washed-up shell and it being a stunning royal color and extra-large to boot!"

"Yes ma'am. The legendary Fran Tatum's masterpieces cannot be matched and unfortunately not duplicated as perfect as hers, but I am certain, if Sir Francis can be reached, he can make your Helena a great looking ring." Cassie watched the wealthy lady scramble toward the door, knowing there would be another pitch for the genuine-original ring, on display in Fran's case.

"My dear Cassondra, just think what a million dollars could mean for this broken down old relic?" Alexandra Templeton gave Cassie a put-on smile. "That one little ring would be of no great lost my dear, now with the excitement over the pass down legend concerning Fran Tatum becoming cooled off rapidly." The arrogant woman raised her eyebrow. "My dear, we wouldn't want the local paper to write up another article disputing this phony legend about Fran Tatum, now would we?"

Jeremiah had taken all he could from this overly proud

woman and he stepped up beside his new friend. "Excuse me ma'am, but I know a threat when I hear one made. You think you can threaten someone by giving in to your threats when they refuse to take a sum of money offered as a bribe?"

"Just who do you think you are sir? I find this little transaction between me and my devoted friend's salesclerk, Cassondra Stevens, none of your business!" Mrs. Templeton stuck her nose up in the air. "So kindly stay out of our business or I shall report Miss Stevens for entertaining a gentleman in the loft during business hours!"

"Look, Mrs. Templeton, I will not let you speak to another one of my customers in such a vile manner! I have my suspicions on to who has been giving that local paper editor all the recent misguiding stories about Fran Tatum so the public's interest in her story will keep them from visiting the gift shop to witness for themselves her amazing heritage."

"You will see how easy it will be when the right person brings the truth to light about this dead woman, now lying decayed in her cold grave." The obnoxious woman swept her hand around the old building. "Wouldn't it be ashamed if Mayor Crib saw fit to condemn this ancient old building?"

"Stooping to blackmail now, Mrs. Templeton?" Jeremiah made his way down the stairs to get face to face with the brazing rich woman. "It would be a shame to have to miss your spoiled daughter's wedding." The young minister remained calm watching the woman's face grow red. "Bribing, threating, and now blackmail, makes for a perfect legal case. You could be paying out that million dollars in legal fees. Madam. In America, no one is above the law and I am a witness as to every word you have said."

"We shall see what my friend Fannie has to say about me buying that old useless ring, just setting up there behind that case." She grunted and stuck out her lips in defiance. "Why, if she were here, I would see you fired young lady!"

The rich customer never knew the owner of the gift shop had slipped inside to hear the entire conversation and the twelfth-generation owner, named Fannie Freeman, didn't like what was said. "I am here Alexandra, and I do plan to do something to my new salesclerk."

A cocky grin came on the wealthy woman's face as she turned to see this new worker's expression when her 'friend' fired her for mistreating her best customer. "Please do darling for she has treated me with total disrespect."

Both Cassie and Jeremiah held their tongues and waited for the shop owner to respond to what she had heard. Her eyes fell on the young woman.

"Cassie, I wish to thank you for standing up for the integrity of this old building that has been in my family for centuries. For your loyalty I intend to give you a raise and promote you to fulltime manager." Fannie turned to the young minister. "Reverend Mitchell, please except my gratitude for standing for what is right and just." She paused, when she noticed what he was wearing around his neck, but she decided to wait for any comments about it until after she got rid of the neighborhood gossip. "Mrs. Templeton, I fill you have gone too far this time and I find your conduct unsuitable for a woman in your position." Seeing she had made the wealthy woman uncomfortable over her bad behavior, the shop owner nodded her head in Cassie and Jeremiah direction. "Maybe an apology is in order Alexandra. Wouldn't you agree, knowing any chance of having Sir Francis design your daughter the Blue-Royal Pearl ring is hanging on it."

"Why of course, I must apologize for my frenzy behavior toward these two refine people." Mrs. Templeton gave a casual wave in the air. "I just got so desperate and the magnificent ring was in reach. This wedding is so important to my precious baby and I want everything to be exactly as she has dreamed it."

"Mrs. Templeton, I was always under the impression that it is the grooms place to give his bride-to be her engagement ring, then follow it up with the wedding band on their wedding day." Jeremiah had conducted several weddings since he began preaching and he was up on all the traditions between a bride and groom."

"Jeremiah is right ma'am. How will the groom feel if he offers her an engagement ring and she exchanges it for another one, more suitable for her rich taste?" Cassie knew by this

32

woman's statement that her daughter was exactly like her demanding mother. "If this man who asked her to marry him has any integrity, he might be a no show at this fabulous ceremony, created just for the bride." She smiled down when she heard the handsome minister say, amen, then glanced up to receive a hateful frown from the brides irritated mother then smiled up at her employer. "Fannie, did you get in touch with Sir Francis?" that statement brought a hopeful look on the rich customer's face as she stood straight.

"As a matter of fact, Cassie, Frank and I spent a lovely few days in Paris and had a marvelous time. There is no doubt that Paris is for lovers." Fannie blushed when she caught the minister's eyes. "It is truly the perfect getaway on one's honeymoon." The shop owner held out her left hand and the small group instantly noticed the large diamond and solid-gold band gracing her slim finger.

"Oh, happy day! Please tell me you brought your new husband back to Marsh Cove?" Alexandra felt like dancing but she knew she must keep her dignity in tack. "Where have you hidden him, my lucky old friend?"

"My charming wife has not misplaced her faithful husband quite yet madam." The very proper British gentleman walked in with flare and confidence and set down two large suitcases.

"Fannie darling, please don't tell me that you have brought this fine country gentleman here in that small studio apartment attached to this antique shop?" the rich customer admired the well-dressed man, standing erect and sporting a fancy walking cane. "My dear Sir Francis, surely you are more accustomed to a large dwelling than a small two-room apartment, with hardly any room for one soul, much less two." She waved her hand with drama. "Why my guest house is bigger than dear Fannie's wee place."

The highly educated man looked over his wire-rim glasses then down at the two large suitcases. "Oh, now I see what you are referring too madam." Sir Frank chuckled along with Fannie. "You just assumed my charming wife and I would be taking up residents in this refine old establishment. I do say, that is cracker Jack!" he reached down to pat the tops of his bags. "These lovely old bags contain my life's trade. The perfect tools for making fabulous bobs and such. My dearest and I have converted her old pad into my work shop and since I purchased the Brower Estate just beyond this quant little village, we shall be taking up residence there."

"Oh, do except my apology Sir Francis for mistaking your tools for your travel bags." She batted her eyes, in hopes of winning the very talented craft artist over. "I simply adore your work and that is why I insisted that my dearest friend Fannie have you to make my daughter a replica of the Blue-Royal ring to cap off her perfect wedding."

"I see! You would have me to make the great Fran Tatum's prize ring." He glanced over and noticed the young couple listening with great interest and gave them a friendly nod before turning his attention back on the wealthy woman. "I may be able to make a perfect copy if, I can find a large royal blue pearl for the inset stone and make sure the lucky young man who will be purchasing it for his bride can afford such a luxurious engagement ring."

"I am certain my team of divers have brought up enough oysters to discover at least one royal blue gem large enough to make my little kittens dream ring." Mrs. Templeton gave a nervous laugh. "Tony, the very lucky man she chose to marry, won't be putting up the money for my baby's dream ring. Her mother and father are taking care of everything?"

The English gentleman's eyebrow went up. "I see. And what does the groom think about being left out of his own wedding." He gave a little grunt. "Will you and Mr. Templeton be going on the honey with your lucky little daughter and her poor groom, or will the three of you just leave old Tony behind, to finish the wedding cake, featuring the magnificent bride standing in the center of her favorite cake and washing down each lumpy bite with the remainder of the expensive champagne."

"Frank, maybe it won't be so bad for Tony if the bridesmaid stays behind to keep him from being lonely." Jeremiah had picked up on the artist's sarcasm and received a big smile from the Brit. "I bet the lovely single lady probably caught the happy bride's bouquet to boot!"

"Who is this remarkable young man?" the famous jewelry maker walked over to shake Jeremiah's extended hand and instantly he spotted the Sacred Cross. Cassie and Fannie held their breath, hoping the great Sir Francis would know to remain quiet about his remarkable find until this conniving woman left the premises. "You look like a man of knowledge, so tell me, have you ever heard of the great Fran Tatum, known throughout the world as the shell lady?"

"Know her? How could I not know the remarkable lady, Sir Franco? I met the dear shell lady last night on the beach, collecting her bucket of colorful shells!" Jeremiah caught Fannie, Sir Franco and Mrs. Alexandra Templeton off guard as they all stared at him, each wondering if he had seen the ghost of Fran Tatum. "Fran had quite a story to tell and that was the reason for me coming by the gift shop first thing this morning. The need to know more about this very talented woman." Jeremiah's attention went on the wealthy customer, who had bragged about the dear woman being cold in her grave and how the public had lost interest in this gifted beach dweller. Never being one to pass around lies, Jeremiah worded his next remark carefully for the overbearing woman who had threaten this remarkable young woman he had instant feelings for and the fact that this old building was worth fighting for, plus the need to defend this beautiful shell lady he had grown to care about deeply. "Sometimes, Mrs. Templeton, we make a poor comment about a deceased member of the family of God, referring to some gossip, living today, having some kind of made-up story concerning the dear shell lady, who's only fault was giving all her money from her jewelry sales to the orphanage for children in Raleigh. It is ugly to gloat over the dead woman being a decayed-cold body when her very spirit still roams the beach at twilight searching for her colorful shells, and perhaps, another royal-blue-oyster, this time to create a matching necklace to compliment the prize ring she made." The young minister noticed the frightened woman, sparked up at the possibility of the wandering spirit creating another Blue royal masterpiece." Too bad spirits from the departed can never create their grand pieces of Jewelry below the clouds of heaven once dead." Jeremiah watched her hope fade. "But the one thing they can do is haunt anyone who tries to ruin their reputation or take what rightfully belong to them."

"A ghost spotting always sparks new interest in a dwindling subject regarding history, Mrs. Templeton." Cassie gave her new friend a wink and the rude customer a knowing smile. "And we can thank you for disturbing her peaceful rest. If I were you or your charming daughter Helena, I would avoid the beach after sunset. The shell lady was gracious with my friend Jeremiah last night, but things might not go so well for the ones that called her up from that cold-dark-grave."

"My dear 'old friend', maybe you had better start glancing over your shoulder now and then, until Fran's spirit grows tired of haunting and decides you are simply not worth her time." Fannie patted her pale face and walked her to the door. "The wedding is still a month away darling, so relax, I am sure my Frank can create a breathtaking royal blue ring for Helena." The shop owner opened the door for her friend, who was looking up and down the beach front. "Now, I wouldn't start worrying about that elderly Fran riding a wave in just to reach you up here, while you're scurrying to your Lexus."

"Oh my! I never considered a ghost surfing, especially an elderly one who lived in the 1700's!" the prim and proper woman quickly laid two-air kisses on either side of the shop owners face and dashed up the walk to her car, as a beach ball blew from the beach and brushed against her arm causing the arrogant women to scream out, and take off into a run.

CHAPTER 6

"Reverend Mitchell, that was quite some story you told that obnoxious stuck-up rich snob!" The Englishman chuckled, just recalling the woman's scared reaction over the minister's made-up story about the spirit of Fran Tatum. "You even had me going there awhile when you claim to have seen her on the beach last evening after seeing what appeared to be the shell lady's most sought-after necklaces hanging around your neck! What an imagination!"

"Mr. Francis, there is one trait that I have held since I was old enough to wag my tongue and that is to never tell a lie. You may be sure, every word I speak is the God's honest truth." Jeremiah noticed the instant change in the friendly man and the seriousness from Fannie Freeman Francis. "I did have the honor of meeting the late Fran Tatum last night, although at the time of our meeting I never knew she had been dead for well-over-200-years." Jeremiah held up the stunning necklace. "Fran hung the Sacred Cross around my neck as she told me to wear it as a symbol of faith. I cannot go into my reasons for needing the angelic message from a much younger Fran Tatum, but I finally feel hope for what I must face."

"This is indeed a mystery Reverend Mitchell, especially since Fran Tatum was buried wearing her necklace." Fannie had heard all the stories past down about the talented jewelry maker and she felt the need to share what she knew with this fine young minister she had heard so many good things about. "I haven't had the chance to witness one of your sermons Reverend, but from all the witnesses who have passed through my shop since you became their full-time preacher, you are very close to Billy Graham when it comes to touching the hearts of your congregation. So, I hope whatever your situation may be, by the good graces of God you will receive what you are after."

"Bless you Fannie. You have a kind heart, so please call me

Joan Byrd

Jeremy" Jeremiah glanced over at pretty girl that gave him butterflies. "And you did right by Cassie. She has helped me a lot this morning, telling me about Fran."

"Then you know the dear lady was buried in everything you saw in her portrait." She smiled when he nodded. "What you and my wonderful helper don't know was why she had never been married, at least to a man. Fran was orphaned when she was ten, much like you were Jeremy, but there was no room for the poor child at the state orphanage so she was sent away to Rome, Italy, where she was placed in a convent with an order of nuns. When she reached fifteen, she gave her life to Jesus and became a nun. Knowing the condition of the North Carolina State Orphanage, she convinced Mother Katherine to send her along with three more sisters to start a new home for unwanted children." Fannie recalled hearing her story many times in order to share the information to interested customers passing through Marsh Cove. "The nuns built their twenty-room orphanage here at Marsh Cove and during her off times, Sister Fran made her trek through the seagrass to the beach and noticed a brilliant-white oyster shell lying at her feet. When she snooped down to pick it up, her attention fell on a large group of tiny-pink seashells lying around the prize oyster. Not having a bucket to placed them in, Sister Fran removed her headwrap and from out of nowhere, a strong ocean breeze swept over her hands causing her nuns headwrap to blow up, swirl around before landing beside the oyster, now standing open, showing off its perfect royal blue pearl, the size of a quarter. It was said, Fran heard the voice of God giving her a message.to become the shell lady and to collect the blue-royal, the pink shells and the healing sticks, that seek safety under the large oyster shell, and make with it a cross necklace and a ring. Place the Sacred Cross around your neck to wear every day throughout your long life. When it comes your time to depart this earth, make thyself a black dress, such as you witness in your dream, and wear both the Sacred Cross Necklace and the Blue-Royal Ring in your burial. There, in the depts. of the earth, they shall be safe until such time they are needed above, where the image of your spirit will walk the beach again." Fannie looked up seriously. "Don't you see, what you said about having a message from God from the one in the image of Fran, had to be God's doing."

"Fran did obey God's command and asked to be buried in both pieces of Jewelry, so why is the Blue Royal not with the Sacred Cross?" Cassie had been listening tensely at her boss's description if the unusual shell lady. "Could someone, have removed the ring before the coffin was closed?"

"I asked my grandmother that very question Cassie and I'm embarrassed to say, the ring on display is not the original Blue-Royal ring," Fannie turned a slight shade of pink. "The ring in the case is a real piece made by the great Fran Tatum and it is almost the exact copy of the first Blue-Royal. After being warn that someone might steal the original ring once placed on her finger unable to defend its safety, the Lord led her to a second oyster shell, housing a big royal-blue pearl so she melted another gold nugget that had washed up on the beach and created a replica. She gave it to my ancestor who had built Fannie's Gift Shop, just to house and sale Fran's exquisite jewelry, all made from God's gifts of the ocean. The fake Blue Royal was placed in Fannie's own personal Fran display, the display you see today, and being Fran's closes friend, Fannie had made a promise to the shell lady. So, on the day Fran Tatum was being prepared for final viewing, Fannie had chosen the last place in line, in order to tell her beloved friend farewell until they met again in heaven. Having the undertaker go behind the coffin to keep him from seeing her place the original Blue-Royal ring on her finger, like Fran asked, when he close it for the final time before placing it down into the ground, he would never know the tears she shed was a decoy to hide the truth."

"So, Jeremy, if the angelic image was wearing the Sacred Cross, which she hung over your neck, did you noticed if she was wearing the priceless ring on her left hand?" Sir Francis had gotten drawn into the mystery.

"I cannot say if Fran wore a ring or not." Jeremiah thought back to the previous night and recalled something he had noticed but didn't think anything about, due to his mind being totally on their conversation. "If you pay close attention to

Fran's black dress you say she was buried in, you will notice how long the sleeves are, falling full around her fingers. The dear lady was so interesting to listen to, it didn't dawn on me until now how her long-flowing sleeves never got wet when she reached down to pick up her shells, even though the surf had just brought the shell ashore and the salty water swirled around her hand and sleeve."

"I think I may be able to help with that unusual happening Jeremy." Cassie knew she had everyone's attention so she continued. "During my studies at Duke, one of my professors suggested that I read The Strange Mystical Experiences of Angelic and Human Spirits. The request directed just for me seemed most troubling then, but now that we are faced with some of the same things mentioned in the book, I count that assignment as a God-given assignment, now recalling how Professor Bulling glanced around as though he were looking for someone, then shrugging his shoulders over telling me to check out this unusual book and casually walking away after dismissing me. There was a section on being around visible spirits and how things that affect us, like rain or snow cannot touch the spirit because it is not physically present, it is spiritually present. I also think Fran's spirit wore the ring on her left hand that stayed safely concealed under the flowing sleeve. She chose to pick up the shells with her right hand."

"Cassie, that is exactly what she did and I think I know why!" Jeremiah enjoyed being with this remarkable young woman and it had made him forget how sick he was. "It is obvious to me and all of you that this Sacred Cross necklace Fran placed around my neck is real and not a spirit necklace that will vanish into thin air. That would mean the Blue Royal ring is also real and had she reached down to pick up a shell in the moonlight with her left hand, the gold band and Blue pearl would have sparkled like the sunrays."

Cassie smiled at the young minister she hoped to know a lot better and felt he was about to share something with her when the demanding customer barged in followed by her employer with her brand-new husband. Feeling let down over any hopes of being alone with Jeremiah for a while longer due to Fannie's most likely plans to take the rest of the week off to be with her new husband and ask Cassie to work through Saturday, she stated "I guess you will be taking a few more days off to be with Frank, Fannie."

"On the contrary darling, you have taken on an extra two weeks as it is, while I was away with my charming husband on our extended honeymoon. We are ready to resume our jobs and Frank has ten clients waiting for a Sir Francis masterpiece including the charming Mrs. Templeton." Fannie gave her loyal worker a reassuring hug.

"I guess I just assumed you love-birds would deed more time for your honeymoon since you offered me full-time manager." Cassie glanced over at Jeremiah and found him focused on her and it please her deeply as she dropped her eyes smiling. "If you need any help with anything before I dash away, I shall be happy to assist either one of you."

"Cassie, you have done more than I could have possibly done myself, so get your things together and I will have your paycheck waiting at the desk." Fannie felt her husband tap her arm and point at the young man waiting by. She caught Frank's message. "By the way Cassie dear, since it is so close to lunchtime, why don't you and Jeremy head up to Lacie's Diner to continue whatever you were discussing when Alexandra Templeton walked into the shop demanding the impossible."

"That sounds lovely Fannie but the Reverend might have other places he has to go." Cassie blushed when she felt the handsome preacher take her hand.

"There is nothing demanding my attention at this moment and I could think of nothing more pleasing than having lunch with such a smart, beautiful young lady." Jeremy smiled down into her green eyes. "Cassie, this would give us the time we need to get acquainted better and take up where we left off before your rude customer came in."

"Then it is settled!" Sir Francis pulled out some large bills and past them to the young man. "Please enjoy your meal on us and we won't take no for an answer. You both were here to guard the treasures from the Foxy-rich mum and for that, we owe you our gratitude. Now, off you two! Cheery-O!"

CHAPTER 7

Lacie's Diner

The host led the couple to a table in the back and casually asked them if it was agreeable.

"This table is perfect Mr. Clark." Cassie had been there a couple times for her evening dinner with Fannie and had learned the host's name. "It is back away from the locals and will give us a quieter place to talk. Thank you." She smiled, picked up her menu and watched the man walk back to the front, then turned to her handsome friend. "Thank you for being tall, dark and handsome Jeremy." She laughed when he got strangled over his water from her sudden flattery question. "I'm sorry, I never meant to make you get choked." Her attention returned to the front desk and noticed the flirty man watching her closely. Jeremiah had noticed the transaction as well.

"Is that man been hitting on you Cassie?" he asked protectively. "Maybe this will convince the big jerk you are taken." The preacher moved his chair in closer to his lunch date and wrapped his arm around her shoulder. Now it was Cassie getting a shock over Jeremiah's sudden affection. "I take it you told Casanova you already had a boyfriend who was tall, dark and handsome, am I right?"

"Guilty!" She glanced up and noticed how serious he was looking at her. "I think you have convinced the flirty host that my boyfriend is real." She blushed, feeling a fluttering sensation fill her stomach and she wondered if he felt the same incredible sparks. "Perhaps we had better look and see what we want."

"I already know what I want Cassie." Jeremiah spoke so passionate, her heart seemed to flip over. His fingers brushed her lips before he turned to his menu. "Now, to decide what I want for lunch." He smiled over the menu. "Since you have eaten here before, what do you recommend lovely lady?"

Cassie took a deep breath before answering the enchanting minister with the most handsome face she had ever seen. "I recommend the Scrimp and Grits Jeremy. The chef makes a fabulous sauce that makes it melt in your mouth and the homemade yeast rolls are the talk of the town."

"Sounds perfect Cassie and just in time for the approaching waitress." He looked over and gave her a wink before adding. "If its alright, I shall order for us." She smiled, giving him a wink and a nod, causing him to laugh out when the waitress stopped and quickly straighten up after recognizing the handsome man and actually seated with a beautiful stranger. "Hello Miss Ross."

"Pastor Jeremiah, I didn't see you come into the diner and with a lovely lunch date." The twenty-five-year-old waitress was a member of Messiah Methodist and like every available woman at the church, she had a crush on her preacher. "I am happy you finally made it to our fine diner." She couldn't stop staring at the lucky woman next to the man she dreamed about having. "I don't believe we have ever met Mrs.?"

"Tonya, Miss Steven is new to the Cove and unless you were off the times she has come inside this diner to eat with her employer, Fannie Freeman Francis, you could not have known my beautiful date works right down the beach from Lacie's." Jeremiah could feel Cassie's eyes watching them converse.

"You work at Fannie's Gift Shop?" she presented Cassie with a fake smile. "I would get totally board standing around that over stuffed shop and wait on an occasional customer looking for saltwater taffy or some cheap nick-tac!" Her flirty eyes turn to the handsome man, who was now growing upset over her obvious jealousy toward the woman he had fallen in love with. "Just how did you meet this salesclerk Pastor Jeremiah?"

"Although it is really none of your business Miss Ross, but I met Cassie at Fannie's terrific gift shop, which is a lot more than you painted it." He purposely reached for Cassie's hand to hold while he talked to the blushing church member. "There is a wonderful antique section up in the loft that features a display of my favorite jewelry artist, Fran Tatum, who died in 1760, leaving a mystery behind and maybe, her wandering spirit."

"There is a ghost in that gift shop?" The waitress swallowed.

"I have heard she has been seen walking along the beach at twilight, collecting shells." He smiled down at Cassie when she gave a soft laugh.

"Jeremy is right Miss Ross and you are quite mistaken by the lack of customers." Cassie gave the girl a real smile, noticed by a happy Jeremiah. "I suggest you read the Morning Sun when it comes hot off the press then glanced down the street and check out Fannie's parking lot." She handed the waitress her menu. Jeremy darling, you may go ahead and place our order. I do believe dear Tonya is getting the eye by her boss."

"Then, I shall place our order beloved before this dear girl gets fired." Tonya turned to see if she was being watched by Lacie giving time for the couple to exchange smiles. "My lady and I will have the Scrimp and Grits and asked the chef to go heavy with the sauce. You may bring us some hot rolls and two garden salads right after you bring us a bottle of your best Merlot."

"A bottle of—" she stuttered as she watched her dream start to fade.

"Merlot!" Cassie picked up his menu and passed it to the stunned girl. "Tonya, even ministers like Jeremy and I enjoy wine, when we are with the right person."

"You are a minister too?" the nosy waitress felt her manager take her arm.

"Please excuse Tonya for taking up your time Reverend Stevens, Reverend Mitchell." The owner gave a polite bow before leaving. "I will bring your wine right out. On the house!"

The rest of the meal went well, and with no more interruptions from the jealous young woman. The couple made small talk, learning about their past childhood and college years. Not wanting the time with Cassie to end, Jeremiah asked her if she would like a stroll down the beach. He had something important to tell her and he knew he must come out with what he was facing before they became too serious over one another.

"Cassie, I have always wanted to know what it was like to

fall in love with the right woman and until now I thought I might never know." Cassie glanced up, now with hope the man she fell so quickly in love with might be speaking about her. His attention was straight ahead so she knew she would be patient and wait to find out. "It is funny how life seems to be empty for so long and you're given a reason to be glad it never happened, but then it appears, right out of the blue and your entire soul cries, why now when I cannot make a life with the one I have fallen in love with?" Jeremiah's eyes dropped down into hers. "If things could be different I would spend the rest of my days on earth with you Cassie, for I am deeply in love with you."

"It all happened so fast and like you dearest Jeremy, the years I searched for mister right seemed to drag along. I believe the Lord made us for one-another and whatever you are facing I feel I am suppose to be apart of it." Cassie gently squeezed his weak hand. "I have noticed how pale you look darling. Does this thing have anything to your health?"

"You are a wise woman Cassie Stevens and so incredibility beautiful. Both outward and inward." He stopped to hold her hands. "If we are to be partners in life, no matter how short, then you have the right to know all there is to know about my dark past and my fatal condition."

"Fatal? My beloved, please do not tell me you have a serious kind of cancer that will steal the one I just gave my heart to, away from me!" tears welled up in her alluring green eyes and she knew to hide them would be impossible. "This dark past you have cannot be any worse than most children of God keep hidden away." Cassie felt she needed to find strength for both of them, so she wiped away the tears and gripped his hands firmly in hers. "Whatever you have to tell me Jeremy, I will forever be at your side to offer my endearing commitment to you that shall never weaver."

"Because of something that happened from my childhood past, I have contracted a rare disease of the blood called Tri-Lexica. The blood cells lose their ability to produce blood so this is why I look pale." Jeremiah could see how much the truth had hurt Cassie as he watched her fight back her tears as she gently pulled away to hold down her uncontrollable trembles. If the young minister hadn't realized just how much Cassie loved him, he could see it clearly now. Now, feeling the need to comfort the woman he deeply loved, Jeremy took her into his arms and held her close, letting her release the held-back tears as she wept. "My darling Cassie, I too felt the full impact of what I heard my close friend, Doctor Bennet Wall tell me but after speaking to Fran last night on the moonlit beach, new hope sprung up inside my heart and I suddenly felt like I can move that giant mountain standing in my way and be healed by the Almighty!"

"How do you plan to descend upon that mountain and overcome this illness that seems to be incurable?" Cassie finally saw a glimpse of hope for the man she had fell in love with at first sight. "What ever you are planning Jeremy, please include me in those plans. I wish to be beside you every step of the way, if you want me."

"There is no question about wanting you next to me Cassie, the problem lies with us being able to get you in on the Holy Lands tour to Jerusalem after I just received the last ticket to go and miraculously being chose to take the cross on the last path to Golgotha." Jeremiah watched Cassie's beautiful face light up with the realization of the importance of going to the reenactment of the Lord's final hours. "According to the angelic Fran, I can find redemption at the cross and the blood of the Lamb, our blessed Savior, will heal my affliction the moment I follow the messenger of Gods instructions."

"Then this thing must be done soon. You said the disease is fatal and your body is no longer producing any more blood, so I can see the urgent need for being healed by faith. No greater time is the Holy week of Christ and no better place to receive your miracle than where our Savior died." Cassie knew any chances to join him on this faith journey would be all but impossible, but with God, all things are possible, like Jeremiah's last-minute ticket and getting the last leg in the cross-pull down the narrow streets of old Jerusalem." Jeremy, I know my chances for getting a ticket on that Holy-Land Tour may be impossible, but I truly believe that if our loving Lord wants me to be there for you, then I will find my own beautiful ticket waiting at my door."

"Cassie, I would love nothing more than to have you beside me during this miracle of miracles. Jeremiah smiled down as he brushed her lips gently with his finger. "It might be a good ideal though if one of us call the tour agency and see if another cancelation just happened to come available."

Cassie laughed softly while she shook her head. "I am truly a firm believer in Miracles, but I know the Lord expects us to do our part to get one." She opened her shoulder bag and took out her smartphone then blushed with embarrassment. "When I really want something superfast, I sort get ahead of myself."

Jeremiah chuckled and pulled his phone from his pocket. "Since you obviously do not know the Tour agency's number, I can call, using redial." He couldn't resist bending down to give her a kiss, and suddenly wished he had more time to prolong his kiss with this young woman he had just given his heart to. "It may be faster this way since they already have all my information." Jeremiah heard the tour agent answer the phone and gave Cassie a wink, then whispered. "Stay hopeful." Then to the lady on the other end. "Good afternoon, Mrs. Ladd I believe. We spoke yesterday about an opening in the Holy Land Easter Tour and I am so grateful for the happy response I received. I have a fellow minister who is a very 'close' friend of mine and I was hoping you may be able to find a spot on this very special tour for her."

"Reverend Mitchell, I am pretty certain that this-year's tour is full but if you can hold on just a moment, I will double check." The operator was very polite and asked Jeremiah to hold on while she checked.

"Mrs. Ladd is pretty sure the tour is sold-out but she is gracious enough to check and make sure." Jeremy glanced upward and closed his eyes, which prompt Cassie to do the same. "Lord, Cassie and I feel in our hearts that it was your plan to bring us together as our heart became one almost instantly. If is thy will that she come with me for my miracle healing through your saving blood, then bless us with an opening. Our hearts will be filled with thy light throughout this journey if we are together. If this is not part of thy plan for us, we will love thee still and praise you always our Savior and King. Whatever you decide, we shall enter into that blessed decision with praises and rejoicing. Not our will blessed Jesus, but thy will be done. Amen." Jeremiah instantly heard two different women echoing his amen, Cassie and the operator, who had come back to the phone in time to hear the preacher's moving prayer.

"Reverend Mitchell, with reverent prayers like that one, I can see why miracles abound every time you need something."

"Does that mean you found an opening Mrs. Ladd?" Jeremiah gave Cassie a thumb's up. "Someone canceled, same as before?"

"Not exactly. I guess we just assumed you would be traveling alone so, when we gave you a newly-wed couple's ticket after they suddenly decided to honeymoon is Paris, France instead of Israel, we couldn't place a stranger with you. Since the ticket is made for two persons, your friend may be the second person on that ticket. You have already paid for the double-ticket so if you don't mind sharing the same room while in Jerusalem, your friend can join you." The tour-agent added. "So, she will know, it is just one room but has two queen-size beds."

"We have been blessed yet again, Mrs. Ladd and you may rest assured we are both mature adults who happen to be ministers as well. This thing is again the Lord's doing and He hath joined us together, perhaps to test our strength to be faithful to our calling and wait for marriage to consummate our joining of the bodies." Jeremy put away the phone and pulled Cassie into his arms. "I have a ticket for two, so if you trust sleeping in the same room with me, then we are going to the Holy Lands together."

"Jeremiah Mitchell, I love you far too much to let our sleeping arrangements bother me. We shall be far too busy getting you to that cross in one piece so you can receive that powerful healing by our Savior.

CHAPTER 8

Reverend Jeremiah Mitchell finally came to terms at what he had to do before he left for Jerusalem, tell his congregation why he had to leave. So, after filling in the sad group about his sickness and his only possible cure being at the foot of the cross at Golgotha, the actual spot the Savior gave up his ghost and died, the young minister continued to comfort the faithful members.

"When the Lord heals me and my faith tells me He will, the blessed Savior may lead me to a new mission I do not yet know." Jeremiah looked out at the tearful church members. "You must not be dismayed, my beloved family, for who knows what may accrue down life's highway. I could return after the mission I'll be asked to perform is finished and if, at that time, you want me to return, I will, with a glad heart. Like most of you here, Marsh Cove has been my homeplace, through both good times and bad ones. Here, at the cove, is where my fondest memories are regarding my devoted mother, gone now for twenty-years." The young minister's misty eyes fell on his parents, who had saved him when he was a runaway and adopted him like their very own flesh-in-blood son. "I could never stay away from Nan and George, who could not have loved me more if I had been their own child. I know my saintly mother was overjoyed to know this beautiful couple took in her little boy to raise, feed, protect and help teach all he knows about God." Jeremiah glanced over at Cassie and smiled broadly.

"I need you to know one more thing before I leave this afternoon. You are aware at how false gossip can start small and after the subject being whispered about becomes something they are not. This is why I am telling you right up front, I will not be traveling alone but with the young lady I plan to marry if all goes well on this trip. It appears my years of searching for just the right woman to complete my life stepped into my life Saturday morning and it was love at first sight, for both of us." Jeremiah held out his hand for Cassie to join him at the front of the church. "Cassie, if you will please join me so my church family can see why I was so taken with you the moment our eyes locked."

Cassie did not hesitate to get up and move up beside the man she had given her heart to and she was astonished by the loving response from the members at Messiah. As she gazed out at the many smiling faces, she noticed Tonya, from the diner, who also had a smile on her face as she clapped.

"What a lovely group of Christians." Cassie fought her emotional tears. "I am sure this must be quite a surprise to all of you to find out about Jeremiah sudden love interest as well as his health crisis that demands our immediate attention. The blessings from our gracious Lord have been pouring in, openings coming available where there weren't any. A ticket for the Easter reenactment in Jerusalem, then to find out that the exact spot miraculously opened for Jeremy to carry the cross from the end of Market Street to Golgotha hill. All this came available to him on Friday, the night before we met. Everything had happened so fast but the moment Jeremy told me about his fatal condition, I felt the Holy Spirit nudge me to go with him for support. We knew everything was completely filled up, same as it had been for Jeremy, but by Faith and the will of God, this beautiful person got in. We felt that if was God's will to bring us together at this crucial time so if it were meant for me to go with him, our faith could move the mountain standing in front of us. The Lord always finds a way to work out any problem standing before us, right sweetheart?"

Jeremiah smiled down at the woman he loved, knowing she wanted him to take it from there. "You see friends, the Almighty God knows everything before hand so he made it possible to have a newlywed couple change their mind about going to the Holy Lands for their honeymoon, so I had a double ticket all the time. Our Lord knows I am a gentleman at all times when it comes to entertaining a beautiful young lady and my beloved also carries strong moral beliefs and that was even before she became at minister herself." The young preacher saw Rob Johnson's hand fly up, and he smiled back at the fifteen-year-old, knowing the young man was a cut-up. "So, Rob, you have something 'cute' to add?"

"Just an honest question Rev. When you marry this really nice lady, will your letters be addressed: Rev. and Rev. Mitchell?"

"I will be glad to answer your question Rob." Cassie gave Jeremiah a smile. "After Jeremy and I get married, we shall be addressed as, Rev, and Mrs. Mitchell. When I receive my own commission, I will be addressed as Reverend Cassondra Stevens Mitchell and my congregation can call me Pastor Cassie." Cassie gave the immature young man a beautiful smile and he swallowed his gum before giving his own shaky grin. "Do you know my various titles now Rob?"

"A   yes Mrs., I mean, Reverend, or a Pastor Cassie." The fresh teen sank down when everyone laughed.

"Now friends, let's not make Rob feel bad." The young minister felt better seeing happy faces on the church family instead of sad faces over the bad news that their favorite minister was so sick. "I, for one, appreciate his faithful wit for making a bad situation a funny one." Jeremiah gathered Cassie's hand in his. "Like I said, we leave this afternoon friends, so we are asking for your non-stop prayers that our Savior heals me from this illness then leads me wherever He wills me to go. Be at peace dearly beloved and know that I leave you in loving hands of my dear father, Reverend George Russell."

Outer Banks Airport

"Son, do you have everything you need?" George and Nancy had drove the couple to the small airport where they would take a shuttle plane to Charlotte Airport and join the Holy Land Tour guide from the North Carolina chapter.

"I have everything packed the tour book suggested, my passport and most important, Cassie." Jeremiah gave his adopted parents tight hugs, then smiled when they turned to give his girl the same affection.

"My dear Cassie, if our boy loves you, then we already

51

have you in our hearts." Nancy could not control her tears. "Just take care of each other."

"Mother is right children. To be at the same spot our blessed Redeemer gave His life for us all, will surely bring this miracle we all have been praying for." George Russell helped with Cassie's luggage. "I too have faith in believing you will come back to us Jeremy, made well and REDEEMED BY THE BLOOD OF THE LAMB!"

"I know when you see your son again, he will be filled with the amazing healing of the Savior's blood and lit with his new mission now waiting near that cross." Cassie had taken an instant liking to Jeremiah's adopted parents and the congregation at Messiah Methodist had welcomed her with love and affection. Suddenly this small town took on a different appearance to the big-city girl who had thought when she arrived that boredom would surely kill her if she had been given a church there and she couldn't pull up her roots and go someplace with more to offer. Now, with Jeremy by her side, she felt a rush of sadness for leaving the charming town as she climbed on the small plane. Cassie knew if Jeremiah didn't get the healing they all hoped for, she could never return without him, the beautiful cove where they met and fell in love.

"We will come home Cassie darling, both of us." Jeremy lifted Cassie's chin and kissed her lovingly then helped his new love in the window seat, before he took the seat next to her "God will give me the strength I need to carry the cross my distance. If our Lord could bare the cross after all the abuse He endured, weary, worn and tired, I can walk the chosen path until I reached that mountain, standing in my way! By faith, the lifted cross will reveal our Savior's image that I alone can see, and I will stand at his feet as Jesus' precious blood runs down to meet me. It is then the blood of my Redeemer will be gathered on my fingers and with prayer and thanksgiving, I will spread the life-saving blood of Jesus on my forehead and be healed. Then we wait to learn what this special mission is and where it will take us."

CHAPTER 9

Jerusalem

The airport van pulled up at the large hotel and several bellhops began to gather to collect the visitor's luggage and show them to their room. One very tall bellhop had two other hotel employees standing next to him holding champagne, a basket of fresh fruit and chocolates. Each person on the tour had been given a card with their room number, so when the tour guide asked the group to hold up the number, Jeremiah pulled out his and Cassie's card. The special welcoming committee gave them a happy smile before stepping up.

"Number 7! The very lucky bridegroom and his extra charming bride!" the bellhop gave them a fancy bow. "It is always my pleasure to escort all the newlyweds to the Hilton's honeymoon suite. We are happy to upgrade your reservation to our grand honeymoon suite, with two bedrooms, the masters king size bed being the choice of newlyweds. There is a spacious room in between with a lovely seated area and small dining table with chairs, should the couple choose to have a romantic meal sent to their suite." Before the couple could respond, the tour guide stepped over to intervene.

"And the lovely couple are just as happy to be here, Mr. Shar." She nodded to the luggage marked 7. "You may show Jeremiah and Cassie to their room so they can get freshened up for our gathering in the Garden Room at seven. We are running slightly behind our schedule due to Israel's strict airport entry check-in. Not that I blame them, being surrounded by the enemy countries."

As the bellhop loaded their things on his luggage carrier, Mrs. Wellington spoke softly to Jeremy and Cassie. "There was not enough time to inform the hotel about the ticket swap my dears, so just enjoy all the extras that come with the wedding suite. They need not know you are not married and merely good friends in search of a miracle."

Joan Byrd

"Then I hope you won't mind if Cassie and I go out on our own while we are here instead of staying with the tour group." Jeremiah knew he needed to have time to search out the place and time for his appointment with the Lord to receive Emanuel's orders. "This visit will be more than a healing Mrs. Wellington. At some point after I have been healed, I will meet up with my Savior and shall receive some mission never before performed."

"Then if this is the will of our Lord Reverend Mitchell, who am I to stand in your way." The understanding guide patted his shoulder. "Just be careful while among the crowd. Many of Israel's enemies are no friend of America either. If you need us for anything, don't hesitate to call my cell. Good luck and God safe keeping."

The spacious hotel suite had more than enough room for the unwed couple, so they had a restful night and were up bright and early the following morning. Palm Sunday had all the visitors from around the world excited for the Holy week celebrations had finally arrived and later in the day, the large crowds would be gathering out side the Golden Gate, between Jerusalem and Bethany to view the reenactment of Jesus riding toward Jerusalem on the donkey. There would be palm branches handed out for the people watching to wave.

Jeremiah and Cassie had found a Christian assembly for morning worship services and attended, happily joining in the well-known hymns of praise for Palm Sunday. They did the usual sightseeing before it grew time for the reenactment and arrived to find the perfect spot to view the Lord's processional.

As the crowds grew larger, the obvious excitement grew. Each spectator had been given two large palm branches to wave when the actors grew near. Jeremiah hadn't noticed the elderly lady who had stepped up beside him dressed in Israelite clothing. As he was looking up the narrow road for any sign of the donkey, the lady spoke up over the noisy of the spectators.

"We must just be patient for the Lord to come." Thinking he recognized the voice, the young minister glanced down to see her smiling up. "Jeremiah, did you know, it was on such a day as today when Jesus rode that colt down this same narrow road we see in front of us?" she noticed his questioning eyes. "You are wondering how I know these things and perhaps" there was a twinkle in her bright eyes. "how I know who you are. Surely you must remember me speaking to you on that beach in North Carolina, just one of God's beautiful states making up His Free America."

"You look and sound like my friend Fran Tatum, but I sadly learned when she lived and died, and assumed I was actually in the presence of an angel." Jeremiah was so caught up with the angel's sudden appearance, he hadn't considered if Cassie had heard them speaking. "Are you here to help guide me?"

"You are very wise Jeremiah, so listen and do as I say." She spoke for his ears only. "You now wear the Sacred Cross beneath your shirt, but for the miracles to begin, you must pull it free, then wait. You will know the moment they happen."

Jeremiah glanced down as he pulled the stunning cross out from underneath his shirt and instantly felt Cassie take his arm. "Oh! Cassie, she is here! Fran, in angel form."

Cassie glanced around him and noticed an oriental couple next to him, then back up at him, confused. "If she was here, she is gone now."

Jeremy turned to see for himself and noticed the angel standing there smiling. "Jeremiah, your sweetheart cannot see me or hear me speak, so you will just have to make her understand why you alone can." With that, the angel disappeared and the couple from Japan smiled up at him.

"Cassie, the angel informed me that I was the only one that can see or hear her." He took Cassie's hand. "She means you no disrespect darling. She asked me to take the Sacred Cross out so the miracles could begin."

"Jeremy, I am here to support you and I do not get discourage over the heavenly attention you are receiving, so please know that your girl is content just to be by your side, should you need me." Cassie reached up and gave him a reassuring kiss, then heard someone nearby call out

"I see the donkey headed this way!" came the voice with excitement. "The Lord will soon reach us!"

Cassie lend over to talk privately to the man she had grown

to love so quickly. "I imagine the people waiting for Jesus over two thousand years ago, were feeling much like we do, only they were probably lined up down on that road instead of back here behind the rock wall."

"They had to be down near the Savior, for the Bible tells about how they would throw the palm branches down in front of him, as well as their cloaks, head wraps and other clothing items while they sang praises." Jeremiah and Cassie joined the rest of the crowd in waving the big palm branches they had been given by reenactment organizers. Suddenly the noise from the crowd around him grew muffled as new-louder praises could be heard from the road below. Standing speechless, the young minister watched bodies appear and connect to the shouting voices. There was no mistaking who those worshipers were and who they were shouting praises to. The actor who had worn a perfect costume for Jesus had been replaced by, the real Jesus of Nazareth. Within a flash, Jeremiah was no longer standing in modern-day, he was taken back 2,000 years.

Jesus was just a few feet away from Jeremiah and he was the only voice shouting out in English as Hebrew, Greek and Latin rang out from the multitude. When the young man noticed Jesus asking that Peter, who led the colt through the crowd, stop a moment, the devoted disciple instantly obeyed, then looked around to see who had drawn his master's attention. Jeremiah, unsure if he could be seen or not, glanced down, closing his eyes. Then he heard the most demanding yet tender voice the young minister had ever heard and he just knew it had to be the voice of the Savior. Suddenly the words Jesus spoke made Jeremiah perk up. Had the Lord spoke clear English in a period of the other three languages. Most Jews spoke Hebrew, and no doubt the Lord was fluent in all Languages at the time He lived as a man on earth. Jeremiah finally looked up when he heard the Lord say his name.

"Jeremiah, your devoted mother gave you a strong Hebrew name as she also had some brother and sister Jews in her family." The Lord knew this would be a surprise for the young minister, never having heard it mentioned. "You need not say a word, my brother, for no one praising me can hear or see you among them. Nor can they see my attention is on someone they could not have known since you never existed until the present. In your weak state the cross will be just as hard for you to carry as it was for me over 2,000 years ago. What blood you have left cannot be spared, should you scrape yourself and bleed. I was extremely weak and weary after losing so much blood before being ordered to pick up the heavy Dogwood cross, and carry it all the way to Calvary Hill." Jesus had paused his ride to speak to Jeremiah and turned to continue His ride to the Temple gate. "Do not be afraid Jeremiah if you wound yourself, thy shalt be healed so you can continue carrying the cross where I will meet you."

Jeremiah instantly stood once again up behind the rock wall over the road, next to Cassie and noticed her sling her head around and let out a relieved breath.

"There you are! What happened to you Jeremy? One minute we were talking about the reenactment being realistic, and after you asked me if I recognized the actor playing Jesus, I turned to answer and you were gone!"

"I know after I tell you where I was, you are probably the only person alive who would believe me." Jeremiah drew in close. "Somehow, I was transferred back 2,000 years ago and was standing down on that road with a large crowd, shouting praises and waving palm branches as Jesus rode passed."

Cassie's eyes grew wide with total excitement. "You saw Jesus? Oh, Jeremy darling, what a beautiful gift. Did He see you?" Cassie paused, knowing how ridiculous that sounded. "Was that a dumb statement? How could Jesus see someone who wasn't there?"

"I cannot explain how Jesus saw me darling, but He did see me and He spoke to me about me having difficulty carrying the heavy cross in my weak state, same weak state He had been in." Jeremiah took her hand and started walking back to the hotel after seeing the oriental couple moving in closer to listen to their conversation. "Cassie, our neighbors back there seemed to be interested in what had happened to me also."

"Do you suppose they saw you vanish into thin air?" Cassie glanced back and noticed they were being followed. "It is

obvious they are intrigued over your sudden disappearance
darling. Even though they are hanging back, that couple is
definitely interested in you. They are following us."

CHAPTER 10

Jeremiah and Cassondra managed to give the interested couple the slip and enjoyed the remainder of the day. After a romantic meal in the hotel's fine dining room, the loving couple went up to their room to plan the week ahead. With several flyers spread out on the shiny walnut table, Jeremiah and Cassie looked over the various tourist holy spots in close distance. Jeremy had opened the bottle of champagne and they discussed which places they wanted to see as they sipped.

"Mt. Tabor was the mount of Transfiguration." Jeremy glanced up "If we take our time walking to the top we can stand were Peter, James, and John watched Jesus's face shine like the sun and his raiment was as white as the light."

"It's where they also witness Moses and Elijah speaking to Jesus, not to mention hearing the voice of God speak from a bright cloud that overshadowed them." Cassie wrote down: Monday, day 1-Mount Tabor. "Maybe we can pack a picnic."

"We shall see if the hotel staff can assist us with packing one for us." Jeremiah gave Cassie a smile, sure of his deep love for her but curious about the many things he did not know about her. Little things he hoped to know to make her happy. "Mount Tabor will take up Monday, so that leaves Tuesday, Wednesday, and Thursday, which must consist of the Upper Room, that is now located in the Church of the Dormition."

"Of course, the room where the Lord had His last supper with disciples and gave them the sacrament of the partaking of the bread and wine as a remembrance of Him giving His body as a sacrifice and the blood for the salvation of sin." Cassie had written in the days and skipped down to write Thursday's must see. "Then we go to the Garden of Gethsemane and see where our Savior spent His last free hours praying to His Father."

"That's right beautiful. Both places are very appropriate for Maundy Thursday." Jeremiah pointed down at the brochure at a stone tomb. "It should be daylight when we go to

Gethsemane, so we can check out the Tomb of the Virgin Mary in the valley below Gethsemane garden."

Cassie made the note and gave Jeremiah a kiss before pointing to Tuesday. "What do you think about touring the nearby towns where Jesus was? Bethlehem, Nazareth, Cana, where He turned the water into great wine" she paused when she heard Jeremiah laugh. "Did that strike my dearest funny? The wine had to be the absolute best wine ever if the Lord Most High made it, right?"

"Like my very wise true-love said, Jesus turned the water into GREAT wine!" The handsome preacher reached over and kissed her, before pouring the rest of the champagne into the flutes. "You may continue with the perfect line-up."

"Capernaum is an absolute must, seeing as to how that was the town where Jesus called four rugged fishermen to 'Come, follow me and I will make you fishers of men.'" Cassie thought for a second. "I guess they will have replicas of Simon Peter, Andrew, James and John's fishing boats there."

"Maybe James and Johns, but brothers Simon and Andrew's boat could very well be preserved for all ages." Jeremiah watched Cassie start to laugh, noticed how serious her beloved was and stopped to consider if he was really serious or preparing to pull her leg. "Aren't you the least bit curious?"

"Well darling, to be perfectly honest, your statement sounded a bit preposterous." Cassie tried to hide her big smile. "Just consider the facts Jeremy. The brothers had, no doubt, been fishing in the same old boat their father fished in, and who knows how many generations back. This family fishing trade on the sea of Galilee could have gone on for years and the old reliable fishing boat had no doubt seen better days. So, you add all those years to the 2,000-years that have past since their time on earth, I cannot imagine a single particle of sawdust left remaining of the old fishing vessel."

"And normally I would hardily agree with my enchanting darling if the Eternal God was not personal involved in the situation." Jeremiah gave her a knowing smile. "It is my belief that whatever the Lord touches becomes eternal and made to last forever, such as this old earth the Holy Creator made many eons ago. As far as we know, there has not been a great change in God's creation unless he found something unsuitable. So, my belief is whatever Jesus touched, built as a carpenter, or climbed aboard, like the brother fishermen's large boat, has all been blessed and preserved for all future generations."

"Sounds like you have got a good case Jeremy, so we just might get a glimpse of the very boat Peter and Andrew took back out and caught more fish than the big boat could hold." Cassie gave the man she adored her prettiest smile. "I would say all those places will take up both Tuesday and Wednesday, if we take our time touring each small town."

"Then it is settled, my dearest Cassie." Jeremiah pushed aside the brochures and pulled her into his arms. "All of the time together will give us a chance to learn more about one another. I just bet my girl is as curious as I am about how we grew up and became the person we fell in love with."

"I would love to know everything there is to know about the man I fell in love with. Little things like, your favorite song, favorite movie, dessert and date night." Cassie reached up to touched his lips and smiled. "As for how many beautiful girls you have kissed before meeting me, I'd rather not know."

"Cassie, it is your lips I long to kiss. No one has ever made me feel the same way you do." Jeremiah's lips met hers and the sudden desire could be felt between them. "You may think it is easy for me to watch you say goodnight and then go into the other room to sleep, but the truth is, I lie awake for hours longing to have you beside me to fulfill the need I desire. Touring this week will make us tired so sleep hopefully will come easy." His hand brushed through her long hair. "I'm just happy my beloved is strong and can walk away."

"Think I'm strong, do you?" Cassie's alluring eyes were serious as she gazed up. "Jeremy darling, it is never easy for me to move from your loving arms to say goodnight, but I can sense your desire for me, the same desire I feel for you, and I know I must be strong, so I say a prayer for strength, receive it graciously, and walk away." She snuggled in his embrace. "Besides, right now you need to save your strength. When Friday comes and its your turn to carry that heavy cross to

Calvary, it's going to take every ounce of strength you have darling." Cassie could not control her tears. "Jeremy, if you get hurt while carrying the cross and start to bleed, then how " she grabbed her trembling lips. "how can you make it all the way if your blood is draining the life out of your body?"

Jeremiah pulled her in tighter, fighting his own tears just watching how much she did love him. "Cassie, the Lord has a plan for me and you are a big part of that plan. I have not felt weak like before since wearing this Sacred Cross, that has a connection to every miracle I have witness. You must not fret my love. I know, without a doubt, I will make it to Golgotha, see the image of our Savior on the cross and reach up to touch the Redeemer's blood and be made whole." Jeremiah gazed up. "Then I shall learn what the Lord has prepared for me to do and you, my beloved, will be a part of our Savior's plan."

"Do you think we shall remain unwed while carrying on the Lord's mission, so we can stay focused on doing His will?" Cassie looked up so serious Jeremiah tried not to laugh. "Look Jeremy, I may be on to the truth here. God knows we are both ministers and He might expect us to be faithful stewards to the job we will hold."

"Are you assuming we will be so caught up in each other if we get married before taking on this mission we could not possibly do our duties to the fullest?" Jeremiah laughed softly. "I rather believe our loving God knows our need for each other Cassie, and keeping us physically apart might prove more distracting than permitting us to get married first, have a much-desired honeymoon, then start the mission with the one we love feeling satisfied that we can go to bed in each other arms at the end of the day."

Cassie had been listening to his common-sense analogy and couldn't resist her chuckle. "Brilliant! That is exactly what my man is, simply brilliant! I only hope our loving Savior feels the same way my charming Jeremiah does!"

"We shall know soon enough darling, but whatever the Lord demands of us, we must do it, regardless to our own personal feelings." Jeremy pulled her close to kiss. "Do you agree?"

"As the Lord holds our first love, we must do what He ask of us." Cassie met Jeremy's lips, then pulled away gently, touching his handsome face. "We serve a loving God darling and my heart tells me before we leave this honeymoon suite, we shall be joined as one. Goodnight my darling, sleep well."

"You too Cassie darling. At least we have our dreams." Jeremiah watched her walk away, closing the door behind her. "Soon, my beautiful woman, you will be walking to my bed." He smiled and went to the other room.

CHAPTER 11

Monday morning proved to be an interesting day. As Jeremiah and Cassondra arrived at the sloping hillside that led up to the rounded top of Mount Tabor, they realized that their plans for making this mountain a one whole day affair was a smart ideal. Even though the Mountain appeared large in the photos they had studied, seeing it in real time let them know just how long it would take to climb the incredible hill. As they prepared for the long climb up to the top, their picnic and extra water had been strapped securely on their backs for whenever they grew hungry or thirsty. Looking around at some gathering tourist, they noticed some from their tour group was there, observing the top of Mt. Tabor with their binoculars. Both Cassie and Jeremy couldn't resist their soft chuckles over what must be the observers only means of seeing the top where Jesus was transfigured and the voice of God could be heard clearly by the nervous disciples that had just witnessed the man they had followed without reservation become transparent and had shone like the radiant sun.

Cassie glanced behind them and noticed the tour guide watching her and Jeremy. "Whoops, it appears Mrs. Wellington caught us observing her group with a slight sneaker." She gave another laugh when her very proper boyfriend glanced down and placed his finger over his lips for silence. Trying hard not to laugh over the situation, Cassie merely raised her shoulders in pretend defeat. "What's done is done Jeremy darling. Besides, from the big smile on Mrs. Wellington's face, we can assume she is not ill with our actions regarding her lazy tour group."

"Cassie is absolutely right about those travelers, Jeremiah. They are perfectly happy to observe from below the mountain rather than make the long way up." The cheerful woman handed the couple a marked trail map for easy excess to the top. "Due to your weak condition young man, this trail is not as hard to make it to the top, where the place where Jesus became transfigured is marked. Believe me, the climb to the top is well worth your time and energy. I have personally climbed up both trails and prefer the B route you will be taking."

"Then we thank you for the B map." Jeremiah checked his watched and knew they had to start climbing if they were going to reach the summit near lunch time. Enjoy the day ma'am and try to get that group active in something. This is a one-time trip for most of them so they need to get involved."

"So far the only thing they seem active in is when it's time to eat." The tour guide gave her own chuckle when Cassie and Jeremiah laughed. "I guess one might say, their mouths are in terrific shape."

"From all the chomping and crewing, laughing and talking." Jeremiah noticed two men seemed to be having some sort of debate over the mountain with all the pointing and arm jesters. "Cassie and I better get moving and let you go tell those confused men that Moses got the Ten Commandment tablets from mount Sinai, not mount Tabor and inform the other genus that this was the mountain of transfiguration not where the Lord spoke his sermon on another mount."

Jeremiah watched Mrs. Wellington looked over and see one man pretending to hold two large stones while the other man had sat down and commenced to pretend preaching to invisible people around him. "Enjoy your climb dears while I go to tell what really took place at the top of Tabor Mountain."

Their slow climb gave Cassie and Jeremiah lots of time to tell some facts about themselves they counted as important for their future mate to know. Cassie's favorite movie was anything with her favorite actor, Gene Hackman. Jeremiah's favorite movie was *The Note Book* and he agreed with Cassie that Gene Hackman was one great actor. The loving couple were amazed to learn they had the same favorite song. "Let it Be Me," first sung by a remarkable couple then years later recorded by the Everly Brothers. They both liked a form of skating, Jeremiah liked ice hockey while Cassie preferred figure skating. Baseball won high marks from them both. They both agreed the very best new author of all times was Joan Byrd, from her incredible array of books, no two being alike. They agreed they couldn't pick a favorite because they enjoyed them all, but Sunset Over Dixie stood out as one of their absolute favorite.

"I have lived at Marsh Cove my entire life and was away for only my classes at Duke to become a minister. My parents were right opposites. My saintly mother Clara clothed me with Faith. She and I attended the same church where I now preach, never missing a single service." Jeremiah knew he had to share everything with the young woman he planned to marry. Nothing good comes from hiding secrets in a marriage. "When I was small, mama would read from the old warn bible I still carry today, and she would explain what the words meant until I grew old enough to know and understand the words for myself." Jeremiah stopped to give her a smile. "I knew from a very young age Cassie that the Lord was calling me to become a preacher." Jeremy's smile fell away as he stared straight ahead, still seeing his father's frightened eyes and hearing him beg for his son to help save him. He stopped and found a rock to rest on. "Let's take a small water break sweetheart. I feel a little out of breath." He noticed Cassie's concern instantly and took her hand. "I will be find Cassie. This is my new normal when I do any kind of physical activity. I just need a few minutes."

"Maybe this wasn't such a good ideal Jeremy darling." She pulled out some water and handed the bottle to him. "We made it half way so that should count for something." Cassie felt a little disappointed, mostly for the man she loved, knowing how much he wanted to make this trip special for them both."

"Cassie, I cannot give up dearest. If I don't get my miracle at the cross this may be my last chance to climb this mountain." Jeremiah managed a smile. "My stopping had more to do with what I need to tell you next than it does with getting too weak to finish. My mama was a roll model for what a perfect Christian should be like but my daddy was an unsaved heathen, a constant drunk, a womanizer, a wife beater as well as a child abuser. He was hateful, stubborn as a mule and strong as an Ox as well as a lazy-greedy bastard." Thinking back to the worse day of his life, Jeremiah gathered Cassie's hand in his and resumed the hike up to the top. "It should have been the happiest day of a ten-year-old boy's life, when his precious mama gave him the gifts he had wanted for his birthday but reasons why he would never get them because money in the Mitchell household was always slim due to one income, from mama's many odd jobs. The old man insisted on his share so he could blow it down at the local bar on booze and women."

"Jeremy darling, sometimes life throws a rotten soul among the true believers for many reasons. It is obvious your mother had seen a different side to your father when she excepted his proposal. A good Christian lady like Clara would never marry a man she did not love and my guess would be that she was a virgin on her wedding night." Cassie squeezed his hand gently. "I might be wrong about my next statement, but I cannot help but believe your wayward father felt love for your mother when he asked her to marry him. Something must have happened to change the man she had chose to marry and it eat away at him until he became the man you grew up to know."

"Cassie, I found out recently that somewhere in my mama heritage we have Jewish ancestry and I believe this is what might have hardened father's heart toward her as well as me." Jeremiah kept his eyes on the path, his inward thoughts hoping this revelation wouldn't change Cassie's heart toward him.

"Jeremy darling, every person on this earth is made up from many different ancestors and it molds us into who we are and what we become." Cassie spoke, with pure love. "I only know from what my parents told me and I dare say from each generation there are many more. From my parents-parents, my grandparents, to their parents, my great-grandparents and so on. I know I have German, Irish, British, Dutch, Holland, Scottish and a dash of American Indian." She smiled when Jeremiah laughed softly. "I guess that's why I love the Moravian Love Feast, Irish Whisky, scones and hot tea, wooden bowls, tulips, the bagpipes, and braids!" she chuckled when Jeremy laughed harder.

"Then, I guess that is why this trip to Jerusalem means so

much to me, because of my Jewish kin!" he paused for a moment. "I was wondering if I had relatives here I know absolutely nothing about." Jeremiah noticed she didn't respond, so he turn to see her staring up and he turn to see what had made her so intrigued. The top of the sloping ridge lay directly overhead and above it was a perfect arched rainbow. "I never saw a rainbow appear without first having rain."

"Maybe the mountain top is getting a few showers amidst the sunshine." She gave her boyfriend a gently nudge to keep moving. "We are almost there and we can see for ourselves."

When Jeremy stepped up on top and gave Cassie a light pulled up, they looked overhead at the bright rainbow, immediately knowing it shone without the aid of showers. Too stun to speak out, Cassie whispered. "Jeremy, it must be some kind of sign from God. What other explanation can there be?"

Jeremiah felt the Sacred Cross grow warm with light and gazed down at it, seeing that it shone with the same intense light as the heavenly rainbow. "My dearest Cassie, it is a message from the Almighty for the cross I wear reflexes the cross I must bear." Jeremiah watched Cassie look down at the Sacred cross that sparkled with life then back up into his eyes.

"Jeremy, did you hear the voice of the Lord tell you this thing concerning the cross you are wearing?"

"I didn't exactly hear the words I said but I can tell you, the words we both heard coming from my lips were spoken by an inward spirit, most like the Holy One that dwells there." Jeremiah knew most women would run from a man who spoke of unknown things. "Cassie, I cannot explain how these things are happening to me, but ever since Fran placed the cross over my head, miraculous things began to happen and up until now I was the only one to witness them. I guess what I'm trying to say to you is, please don't run away from me due to all these strange things happening."

"Run, from the man I gave my heart to! Run, from the love of my life just because the Lord is revealing things to you wherever we go that He once was!" Cassie gave him a gentle hug, always careful not to hurt him. "Did I not tell you that I would stand beside you throughout this healing journey

68

Jeremy? You have nothing to worry about where I am concern my love because whatever you must face I will face with you and if I could help bear the pain you must endure to reach that deadly hill of Golgotha, I would do it gladly. Dearest, shouldn't our immediate love for one another prove that this too was a special gift from the Almighty, when neither of us expected to find love that beautiful morning and it found us and made us one, together, forever."

"I love you Cassie Stevens and to become one with you cannot come fast enough. But, I must be made complete first and come into the blissful union with the strength I once had, to defend, protect, and shower you with all the love a man can give his woman."

The wind blew around the loving couple as a soft voice came from the sudden white cloud that rose above the rainbow. "My beloved, this sacred spot is where I revealed my glory to Peter, James, and John, and where I reveal to you, Jeremiah, that as soon as My Redeeming Blood has cleanse away your illness, what I have planned for you to begin, but this beautiful mission will not begin until you and Cassondra join hands in Holy Wedlock. It is my desire that you take a wife to be your helpmate and a source of companionship. Be fruitful and when the time is right to bare children, you shall be well please with the gifts that fill your home and hearts. Be at peace my beloved, until we speak again." The wind blew up around the cloud-filled rainbow and it vanished.

Jeremiah and Cassie watched the blue sky overhead recalling what the Lord had told them, then gave each other a warm embrace, knowing their wedding was only a few days away. They pulled their backpacks off and prepared the picnic. After Jeremiah gave a moving blessing, he and Cassie enjoyed their quiet lunch on the top of Mt. Tabor.

CHAPTER 12

The next two days were packed with special tours to Bethlehem, Nazareth, Cana, and Capernaum. Many of the original landmarks and dwellings were gone but various replicas had been erected in perspective locations. The Inn in the town of Bethlehem had been restored from the few stones that remained from the original and the stable where Joseph and Mary had been taken, was actually a large cave cut out from large rocks for holding the Inn Keepers cow, a few sheep and a donkey. The wooden stalls and rafters were obviously new wood and the only thing original to the rustic stable was one small manager, sacred and holy, touched by the baby Jesus, God made flesh to dwell among us. Preserved for all time behind musicum glass to keep it protected.

Nazareth had been completely rebuilt from the ground up. Expeditions had been carried out over what was thought to be where the tradesmen worked and sold their products. Those talented men and women who set up the shops along Market Street. From Silversmiths, Spinners of wool and flack, the Tin Smith, the Blacksmith, the Potter and the Carpenter, who was gifted with making anything from wood or stone.

Among all the venters working along Market Street, there was only one left who will be forever remembered, but it wasn't for his great skill at being a carpenter it was who he was the earthly father too. Jesus is the Son of the Almighty Father, and the Virgin Mary was His chosen mother. Joseph, the humble carpenter was set to marry Mary when God the Father, placed His Son inside her, so after being told by the Angel Gabriel that Mary, the young woman he was to marry, was indeed the chosen one of God, Joseph married Mary and Jesus, the Son of God, became his earthly son to watch over and teach Him as his own child.

After the expediters did a through research for what they assumed was Joseph's Carpentry Shop. They built what they assumed it might look like over 2,000-years-ago at the bottom of Market Street. It would have made sense since the Carpenter's business included his sons when they got old enough to learn the building skills. The young apprentice would learn the craft and be bumped up to junior carpenter, then skilled Carpenter. There are a few finished works of art behind musicum glass thought to have been made by Jesus. The house of Mary and Joseph was thought to be next to the Carpenter's shop with a rather large back yard in early AD to have a vegetable garden, a barn to house the donkey and milk cow, for the ever-growing family after the baby Jesus was weaned from his mother's milk.

Again, the loving couple had set out on their own in a rental car and a tourist map. Besides reading about the various places, Jeremiah and Cassie had always managed to be near a tour guide describing each building and plot of ground that could have been used for different things. Bored with some of the tourist questions, Jeremiah took a few steps back to take in the carpenter's shop and instantly heard a wooden hammer banging on what sounded like a peg. As he stared at the spot where the sound came from wondering if the historic park had a sound system hidden somewhere near the worktable, Jeremiah witnessed a man standing at the table in a fuzzy haze. His undergarment was a dingy white robe and over it appeared to be a rustic brown apron, tied around his neck and falling to his knees. Just as he suspected, the mature man with dark hair and a well-kept beard, was striking his wooden hammer on a peg, that fitted perfect into the stool he was working on. So astonished over seeing Joseph, Jeremiah never saw Cassie step up until she touched his arm, causing him to jump and the image disappear.

"Jeremy, I didn't mean to startle you darling but you looked as though you were seeing a ghost." She reached up and touched his forehead. "You looked so pale I grew concern that we might be doing too much for the condition you're in."

"Cassie, I am fine, darling." Jeremiah looped his arm over her shoulder. "You are an angel and I love you deeply, but the fact is, you did startle me just now. I was so caught up with what I was witnessing I never heard you stepped up. I noticed you seemed interested in those questions so I slipped back to look around at the spot where Jesus grew up."

"I admit this spot is the most interesting place in Nazareth." Cassie looked at the spot where her beloved had been staring. "I guess you were imagining Joseph working alongside of a young Jesus, right?"

"I never saw Jesus with Joseph darling and I did not have to imagine him when the real Joseph appeared before me after I heard his hammer striking a peg on something that turned out to be a great-looking stool." Noticing how quiet Cassie had grown, the handsome preacher glanced down to see her big eyes staring at the workbench where he had just witnessed the past. "Don't ask me how it happened that I was privilege to return once again to the past of over 2,000-years but I believe it has something to do with the mission waiting for me to begin and the fact that I wearing the Sacred Cross out like Fran ask."

"Jeremy, if returning to the past is something only you can witness, then what will I be doing all the time you are taken back?" Cassie finally shook her head, knowing she was wasting her time trying to get a small glimpse of the carpenter busy at work. "Waiting for my charming husband, tired of cleaning, reading and watching for any sign of your return?"

Jeremiah could not resist his chuckle when he pulled the clever woman in his arms. "My adoring Cassie, I truly believe you will be anything but bored and I do not think for one second that our loving God will keep two-love birds separated for any length of time." He took her hand and started walking. "Just keep the faith darling. We both know how quickly we grew attached to each other and found ourselves instantly in love. So, there's no doubt that God brought us together with the intended purpose to work closely side-by-side, whatever the mission, wherever it takes us. If it requires time travel, then we shall go together, for we will be made one."

Cana was nothing like the time of Jesus and when he turned water into wine. A large plot of ground was marked to indicate where the wedding feast took place and where Mary was there with Jesus as guest when they ran out of wine. Jeremiah never saw anything from the past in Cana so they moved on until they came to Capernaum and found the Sea of Galilee where the two-sets of brothers fished for six days a week and rested on the Sabbath. The couple could tell Capernaum was still a fishing village and one of the fishermen led them to the old wharf and pointed out two large rustic boats, floating next to the ancient pier.

"There they rest, the old relics everyone comes here to see. The one nearest us is thought to have belong to James and John and the larger vessel belong to Simon Peter and his brother Andrew." The old fisherman gave a hardy laugh. "There is no doubt both boats are old mind you, but can you tell which vessel dates back to over 500-years while the other one goes back a whopping 2,000-years?"

Jeremiah and Cassie exchanged glances before the young preacher spoke up. "It is definitely accurate that the fishing boat closes to us was well built 500-years-ago, and a replica of James and John's vessel while the bigger boat is the real deal. Jesus went aboard the large boat to speak to the crowd then after sending them away asked Simon Peter to take the boat back out and they would catch fish."

The old fisherman gave the man who seemed sure of himself, a hard look. "You sound mighty sure of yourself mister." He paused to see they had drawn a large crowd, so he wanted to prove he knew more than this outspoken American. The fisherman looked around at the listening people and gave a cocky grin, thinking he was about to make this tourist appear ridiculous. "It would be impossible for any wood to outlast that many years. I grant you, old thick lumber can withstand a good many storms and continual floating in sea water but nothing that grows on this old earth can resist the ages of time. Case in point, check to your left and you will see the fishing boat grave yard. Many of them date back a 100-years or so but Mother Nature finally claimed them and one day soon, she will turn both Historic boats into rotten timber and their rotten hulls will rest in the old graveyard."

"Your town has a priceless piece of history, lovingly reserved by God Himself and you sir cannot see the gift that still sits in Galilee, just as it did when Jesus touched it and made it eternal." The laughter had died away as every eye turned to observe the actual fishing boat belonging to Simon Peter and Andrew's family and considered the truth in this frail man's words. Without saying another word due to the sudden uproar just out around a half-mile in the sea, Jeremiah moved closer to the shoreline and gazed out. Cassie had seen her fiancé's reaction to what must have something to do with the biblical encounter that happened over 2,000-years-ago right here at the very spot. As she watched, now along with the large crowd that had gathered, she could tell Jeremiah's Sacred Cross was revealing something that only he could witness. The old fisherman gave a hardy laugh.

"I can say one thing for your husband lady, he is either crazy as a Loon or the best actor I have ever seen!"

"Mr. Daniels, Reverend Jeremiah is neither my husband, crazy or an actor." Cassie sudden grew aggravated over this man putting down her beloved and she was ready to defend him. "This wonderful man of God is my future husband, a witness for the Almighty and at the very moment seeing what he has been believing because, it is the will of Jesus our Lord that Jeremy sees for himself the past life of Jesus as well as the present life with Him!"

"You are joking, right?" the man howled out in laughter. "You expect me and all of these educated adults to believe that story?"

"I can easily believe what I cannot see sir, because my trust comes from my Lord! I also believe these lovely people are here today because they too are followers of Jesus Christ and desire to walk were He walked and hope to feel His Mighty presence wherever He was. I" Cassie paused, titled her head then whipped her head around to where the noise was coming from. She grabbed her trembling lips as she whispered. "I can hear the excited voices out in their boats! The splashing water, like   fish! Hundreds of fish splashing!"

The old fisherman bent over double laughing. "What an act!" his laughing began to die away when he noticed the crowd was not laughing but instead the amazed faces moved up beside the outspoken young woman who had said such moving words. "Ah, come on folks, not you too! I have seen a lot of things in my life but this one beats them all." He paused to listen to what was being said and the fact that not a one of them was listening to his ravings anymore. What was out there that had them all so captivated? He gazed out at the empty sea and shook his head, his long-white hair frazzled from the sea breeze. "Jehovah, what can they see that I cannot? Have I not been a faithful Jew?"

Jeremiah had been observing the big fishing boat out in the water as the fishermen struggled to lift their full nets into the boat. He could hear men's loud voices calling to the shoreline for James and John to bring out their boat because the amount of the catch was more than their boat could hold! The loudest voice called out from the hull and Jeremiah knew he was looking out at Simon Peter. A strong man with rugged handsome looks and with an incredible sound that could be heard a half-mile away.

"JOHN, JAMES! GATHER YOUR SEACREW AND GET YOURSELF OUT HERE BEFORE WE ARE SWAMPED WITH THIS DRAUGHT! THERE IS ENOUGH FISH FOR EVERY FISHERMAN IN CAPERNAUM!"

The sound of another vessel could be heard making its way out by the hard driving oarsmen thrashing their paddles through the deep water. When the second set of brothers reached the spot they quickly let down their nets and they were immediately filled with fish. The noise died away when both boats had taken on all they could hold and Jeremiah could tell everyman from both fishing boats were staring at the One who had ordered Simon Peter to take his boat back out and put down the nets. Even from the great distance, Jeremiah could see the Lord Jesus rise to His feet and he could hear His words clearly.

"This day you have caught many fish and did so well, but now you four, Simon, I name Peter, Andrew, your brother, brothers James and John, it is time to believe what the prophets have told you, to learn the Gospel of your Lord and to leave this life and trade with your fathers, then follow me and I will make you fishers of men!"

Jeremiah had heard the large crowd behind him grow quiet while he watched the fishermen's total confusion on the water and concluded that they too were hearing the excited fishermen pulling in the large number of big fish that had miraculously appeared when the Lord gave the signal to stop the boat and put down the nets. During all the time that was happening, Jeremiah was also privileged to hear the old seaman's words to God and he instantly knew why this man could not believe. The Jewish man had never excepted the fact that Jesus Christ was indeed the Son of God."

"Jeremiah!" the young minister looked out at the fishing boat and noticed Jesus was facing him while the men were bringing the big boats in. "This is your first mission my son, to show this old fisherman I am truly His Savior. This brother has been a faithful Jew but the way to the Father is by me, for I am the way, the truth and the life! Brother Jude does not have many more days to enjoy the fishing he rises for so we must give him a reason to believe. I now rest in Simon Peter and Andrew's fishing boat that is loaded with many large fish. I count on you, my brother, to do the talking and I shall throw you the miracle that will convince the strong headed man of the sea my truth!"

As the crowd wandered around discussing what they had heard, Jeremiah caught the eye of the confused fisherman. "I see even with the excited crowd that heard the fishermen's voices ringing out over the large amount of fish that could be easily seen by me and heard by my beloved Cassie and these devoted Christians, you still hold doubt in your heart brother Jude." Jeremiah could tell by the man's uncertain stare that he was wondering how this stranger knew his God-given name. "I see you cannot understand how a man you just met knows your first name when it was never shared with any of us. All you told us was, I am Captain Daniels, the oldest and most efficient tour guide in town and by the sea and best darn fisherman in the whole of Capernaum."

"Yes sir, that is exactly what I told you, so how do you know my first name and that is only called out in the temple on our holy Sabbath?" the old salty fisherman narrowed his eyes. "And what kind of sorcery did you use on all those poor

Redeemed by the Blood of the Lamb

disillusion Christians who believe in this false Messiah?'

"Jude, surely after all these years you have wondered about this man called Jesus. You must believe what the prophets foretold about a virgin conceiving a baby by the Holy Spirit, who was to be the Son of God. For unto us a child is born, unto us a son is given and the government shall be upon his shoulders and his name shall be called wonderful, councilor, the mighty God, the everlasting father and the prince of peace! Isaiah spoke of how He would be contemned by leaders of the church, beaten and crucified for our sins. The lamb without blemish! The lamb of God!" Jeremiah could feel the man's anxious inward battle and knew his heart was moving in the direction of light and truth. "Jude, your life has been one with the desire to fish and if you had trusted the prophet's words, all those who spoke about Jesus, you too could have heard the hundreds of fish moments ago splashing out there. Out there where the Lord still waits for his brother Jude to believe in Him." Jeremiah noticed the old fisherman's eyes grow misty with tears as he gazed out once more at the empty sea.

"It 'twas Jesus that told you what my name was, wasn't it?" Jude waited for the young man to nod. "You have found out my deepest secret Reverend. I find myself on Holy Sabbath listening to this same prophecy being read by Rabbi Levi and my mind wonders away to that crucifixion and how Isaiah describe the event exactly like the prophet's prophecy." Jude Daniels blinked back his tears. "I've been living with a guilty heart for trying to remain a loyal Jew while wondering if this good man named Jesus was really the Messiah we have been waiting on for so long. Jeremiah, help this poor old stupid fisherman know how to believe without being disowned by my people?"

"Someday all men, Gentiles and Jews, will know that Jesus Christ is truly the Son of God and no man or religion should stand in your way if you choose to believe in Jesus, that He is your Savior and that He died on that cross knowingly, by taking the sins of the earth upon Himself, the only one born that was sinless and perfect! Jude, Jesus died for you on that cross, same as He did for me and everyone standing with us this day. All

77

that is required of you is to believe that Jesus Christ is the Son of God and that He died on that cross to take away your sins. Then confess your sins to Jesus and asked his forgiveness and live your life according to His written word!"

"I'm not afraid anymore to confess my sins to the one that gave His life for me in such a painful way." Tears rolled down Jude's weather-beaten face. "I do believe in you Jesus Christ and I know and have known for some time that you are without a doubt, the Son of God! Take my many sins my Savior from me and cleanse me with thy pure loving blood, and forgive this old fisherman!" His eyes fell on Jeremiah, who had tears in his own eyes as did Cassie and every soul listening. "I can see you Lord in your loving servant Jeremiah and I thank you and praise your holy name for leading him to me." Jude's old eyes looked out hopeful that he might hear the splashing fish, but assumed by the crowd and Jeremiah now giving their attention to him, the heavenly vision was past. "Son, do you think Jesus heard me?"

Jeremiah heard the Lord tell him to lead Jude to the waters edge and he happily obeyed "Jude, you may see for yourself. I believe the Lord has a surprise for you, some gift to show you that He heard every word you said." The young preacher smiled down at the old man as he stared with the excitement of a child. Then Jeremiah looked out to see the Lord smiling at him and again he was the only one to see Jesus. "We are ready Lord." He heard Jesus say, 'both hands for the catch', then tossed him a big fish!

CHAPTER 13

On the way back to the hotel in Jerusalem, Jeremiah and Cassie discussed Jude Daniels reaction over the Lord's sacred gift to the old fisherman. Cassie gazed from the small window in the rental car, recalling what had happened moments ago.

"Jeremy darling, when I noticed the old fisherman's reactions as he gazed out at the same spot where I and all those listening to the excited voices of men shouting to cast down every net before one very loud bilious voice shouted out 'ENOUGH! PULL UP THE NETS IF YOU CAN AND PRAY TO THE GREAT JEHOVIA THEY DO NOT RIP APART', I had assumed he was hoping to hear what we had heard until I saw his tired eyes grow wide with wonder."

"Cassie, I believe Mr. Daniels was privileged to see what I was witnessing and this is why he became amazed to be witnessing for himself the One he just confessed to moments before." Jeremiah reached over to touched her hand resting on the middle armrest. "Jesus was waiting at the helm of the big boat for me to speak to Jude, knowing that he had been struggling with doubt over the Jewish belief that the Messiah had not come yet when all the evidence made believing that Jesus was indeed the true Messiah was right in front of them. The old testament prophets had foretold the coming of the Messiah and actual facts concerning His birth, His life on earth and His death, like who was responsible for ordering his crucifixion. The leaders, the scribes, Priest, and Pharisees." Jeremiah remembered Jude's response when Jesus lifted the large fish in the air. "Jesus was preparing to throw a big fish across the Sea of Galilee to my outstretched hands. By faith, I had no doubt that fish would land directly into my hands."

Earlier at the Sea Dock

"Jude, my beloved brethren, I heard your prayer and saw it came from your heart so I forgive you of all your sins and welcome you into my fold. I allowed you to see not only me, your Lord and Savior, the Messiah who has come, but also to witness four of my beloved disciples, Peter, the loud one, Andrew, his brother and brothers James and John and despite what you have been told about their fishing boats, now retired and tied to the same dock from 2,000-years-ago, both boats are the real thing, reserved for eternal time."

"Lord?" Jude's voice was shaken from being nervous. "Do not get angry with this old weather-beaten fisherman, but how come the smaller boat tied up here with the older one, looks a lot newer?"

"I will not get angry over a legitimate question. One which any normal human would ask." Jesus waited patiently, fish held firmly in midair. "There is a reasonable explanation Jude for James and John's fishing boat to appear newer. Their first family boat had been struck by lightning and the old timbers went up in flames and was a total lost. So, the reason it appears newer now is because it was brand new when I arrived and Peter and Andrew's old boat had been in their family for 500 years."

"So, that's where the number 500 years came from." Jeremiah had been listening and recalled the old fisherman asking him to guess which boat was built 500-years-ago, and the young preacher had obviously picked the smaller boat. "I guess as the story was past down from one generation to the next, the real facts got lost somewhere in translation."

"Exactly Jeremiah, now hold your hands steady and I shall toss this large fish, caught over 2,000-years-ago, across the Galilean Sea where it will pass through time and age until the present. It is an ancient gift from me to my beloved brethren, Jude, sent alive and preserved for all time." Jesus tossed the squirming fish through the air and it easily found its way to Jeremiah's outstretched hands.

PRESENT TIME

"When I caught the fish, it had turned to stone, yet every feature from its head to its tail, was visible and perfect. The brilliant colors still remained and the eyes shone like a moonlit night and appeared as though they could see me observing it."

Jeremiah had pulled in the parking deck at the hotel and turned to face the woman he had fallen in love with so quickly. "Jude was almost speechless when I handed the grand gift to him and all he could say was:

"I'll share it with my people when I retell my miracle and help them to see what I have seen. God bless you son. THE MESSIAH IS ALIVE!"

"Then he raced away, the most energy that dear soul has felt in years."

"It was truly a wonderful gift for all of us who could hear past conversations and the sound of hundreds of fish springing from the deep water." Cassie leaned her head on his shoulder, weary over the long day touring.

Thursday Morning: 10:00 a.m.

Since Mrs. Wellington had already lined up the group for the Jordon River baptism, Jeremiah and Cassie went along to renew their spiritual cleansing. A large crowd had gathered on the bank of the Jordon, at the assumed spot where John the Baptist baptized Jesus over 2,000-years-ago. There was a sense of reverence felt by the large group and any conversations were kept low, out of respect for the Holy event that happened there.

Two ministers waded in the river to administer the baptisms while another man dressed in biblical clothing got the crowds attention when he spoke on a portable microphone. "Good morning, fine people. Welcome to the Jordon River, to be baptized in the same manner as Jesus Christ at this very same spot. We know this to be true because this is the only spot on this river where a large number of people wishing to be baptized can find easy access to the water. Look around and you can see the land above the river bank is flat, to accommodate those who are waiting to come down. The river bank slopes down gently at this spot on the Jordon where elsewhere the bank is steep. This is also the safest to wade in for it drops gently and the depth is shallow in the middle so the one being baptized can easily stand up once baptized. Each group has been given a letter starting with the A group and I have asked all guides to line their group up in whatever order they wish. We ask for your patience while others get their baptism and feel free to look around if you choose. Just don't wander off too far or you might get lost in the tense wilderness that Jesus wandered around in for 40-days while fasting. If you walk to your left it begins about two-tenths of a mile that way. If you choose to check it out you can get the full gist of what lies out there by looking across the vast desert ground." The man looked out and saw the ministers were in place to begin. "Group A, Mr. Clark, you may send your group in, keeping them in a straight line."

As group A started in, Jeremiah asked his guide what letter she had and after learning she had the letter J, the young minister knew the tenth letter was the last group so he had time to check out the opening to the wilderness.

"Mrs. Wellington, it appears this will take some time waiting, so with your permission, I would love to check out the wilderness."

"If you promise not to get too ambitious and travel inside. That desert can look deceiving Jeremiah and one can get easily turned around and before you know it you're lost inside the vast-sometimes deadly place." The tour guide knew the common-sense preacher would not to tempt fate but being responsible for her group she had to put the warning out there for anyone else who was anxious to see where Jesus was tempted by Satan. "You might not find your way out as easy as the Lord."

"You are a wise woman Helen and I never intended to go inside that wilderness." Jeremiah felt Cassie take his hand. "Unlike Jesus who could do anything He set His mind on doing, I would probably get lost after the first hill, since everything looks exactly alike inside a desert."

Noticing Cassie clutching her fiancé's hand, the friendly woman asked. "Will you be taking Cassie with you, reverend?"

"You bet I will Helen." His eyes fell on Cassie. "You cannot be complete when your other half is separated from you, now can you?

"Enjoy yourselves, but watch the time, be back in 30 minutes." The understanding guide waved them away.

The Wilderness

"Have you ever seen such a dreary place?" Cassie lifted her binoculars up to view the distance desert. "It appears to go on forever, much like our deserts out west. Just imagine how Jesus must have felt, alone in that barren land until the angels showed up."

"Just imagine starving yourself out there were there had to be creepy crawly things and knowing you would have to lie down to sleep, never knowing if you were safe." Jeremiah stopped talking when somewhere inside that wilderness a strange howling wind could be heard. "Cassie, do you hear that devil of a wind?"

"It sounds like something out of a horror movie." She shivered at the demonic sound. "Jeremy, I wonder if Jesus heard that same sound before the Devil tempted him?"

"It does sound evil." Jeremiah checked his watch. "We better start heading back. I wouldn't want to miss being baptized."

"Jeremiah." Came the voice just inside the wilderness. "Son, you need not get baptized again for you have already pleased me." The couple exchanged glances as the voice continued. "Step inside with me Jeremiah, so that we may speak about my plans for you."

"The plans are to be given me after I am cured. This is what you told me and I know you always tell the truth, so I shall wait." Jeremiah didn't feel right about the voice, the same voice he had heard many years ago, when he was ten.

"Jeremiah, are they not my plans to give and if I choose to give them now instead of later, then should you not obey your God?" came the same demanding voice, far different from the voice of the Lord Jesus. "Do you remember my helping you many years ago when you were just a mere boy and saved you from your angry father?"

"I do recall your voice offering to help me and asking me to stay still until my father grew close enough to strike with the baseball bat my saintly mother had just given me for my 10th birthday." Jeremiah, now grown and more aware of how the devil works, knew who he was having this conversation with. The young minister knew Lucifer would come to Christians pretending to be Jesus Christ and try to fool them by pulling them into his evil trap using the words relating to those of the Savior. At the end, Lucifer would be so perfected in his impersonation of our Lord. This evil fallen angel would fool many people, including the followers of Jesus, if they were not wise to his deceitful treachery. "I also recall a strong force take hold of the bat and lifting it over my head, then come down with inhuman strength, smashing my bat against the side my father's head, causing him to be disoriented."

"Jeremiah, my brother, you forgot what really happened, being traumatized by your mother's death at the hand of your drunken father." The voice remained calm, deception practiced for many centuries. "Someone who has been traumatized will become defensive and their anger will intensify so rapidly, even a small child at ten can possess inhuman strength and easily take down the enemy badgering them. Son, I had no part in what happened to end your father's tragic life, it was your forceful blow that created his downfall."

"I beg to differ, for I remember well what happened. I was much too nervous to lift that bat with the force it swung up and came down, making that horrible cracking noise." The scene flashed before the young preacher's eyes. "I recall your voice grew different and I remember when my father's facial expression changed when he begged me to help him. I could feel my emotions taking a different turn and I started to move toward him but something was holding me down. Then as father stumbled back closer to the window, I noticed it had been opened wide, where it had been closed earlier. My eyes locked with my teary-eyed father and I can still see his hand, outstretched to me as he pleaded with me to save him. My heart felt like it was in my throat as I fought to run and help him, but I was held securely in place as I heard you say, 'Do not trust his words Jeremiah, he only means you harm. Remember what he did to your precious mama." Jeremiah had lost all count of the time and 30 minutes had just past but Cassie, alert herself as to who was calling from inside the wilderness, knew the man she adored was recalling new truths to that horrible night in his young past. "I know the truth now! It was made clear when my father grew close enough to the open window to see what was waiting for him below! The same evil being that willed the locked window to unlock and open!"

"Son, you are imagined things. I was there and remember the window was opened the entire time." Came the all-to-sure voice. "Jeremiah, I recall your precious mother had mopped right before you came home and opened the window to help dry the floor. Besides, you were just a kid, you could never have saved the drunken man."

"Nice try Lucifer, but there are cracks all in your deceitful lies. My 'precious mama' left that morning when I did and after taking me to school she went to work at Doctor Greens offices until they opened their clinic at ten o'clock, then she went straight to ACE CLEANERS where she ironed clothes until she had to pick me back up from school. You see, my mama was never there to mop so in reality it was one of your demons that opened the window and was waiting to collect my father after he fell to his untimely death."

"Think you are clever Jeremiah Mitchell?" the cocky voice grew loud. "Why do you assume your drunk father's death was 'untimely'?

"Because I know cold-blooded murder makes it so, Satan! God has chosen a time for everyone to die and my father's death was not of His choosing! "Jeremiah felt Cassie draw in close and remembered their time was probably over. "

"Your GOD, this JESUS, who controls everyone's lifespan, would never take much thought of losing one soul, wasted and lost to His perfect way over his young prodigy's life. You killed him in self-defense and I am certain YOUR SAVIOR WILL FORGIVE YOU!"

"I will not be late for our baptism Lucifer so I will just say this one more thing." Jeremiah had heard Mrs. Wellington ring her warning bell. Five more minutes until line up. "My father had asked me to help him, then he asked me to save him. Yes, he was afraid, but it wasn't because he was dying, it was because he was dying without the Savior's forgiveness! My daddy wanted what mama and I had and he had been too proud to asked for our help. In his desperate drunken state, he hit mama and shoved her across the floor, but I know now he never meant to it to kill her. He just wasn't aware of his strength," the young preacher stared out unafraid. "You killed my daddy because you were afraid you would lose his soul and that is why you ruined his evening at the bar and made him come home early so you could wait, place anger inside him so bad he would push my mama hard enough to break her neck, then you pretended to help me while helping your own evil self! If there was a way to bring my daddy back, I would help him let Jesus save his soul like he wanted me to!" Jeremiah took a tight grip on Cassie's hand and walked swiftly away, back to the Jordon River.

CHAPTER 14

Jeremiah and Cassie moved swiftly to reach their group just in time and instantly apologized to their leader who gave them an understanding smile.

"Sometime things can happen unexpected darlings to distract you and I understand how you feel about the need to take in everyplace Jesus walked." Mrs. Helen Wellington had noticed how flushed they had appeared and wondered what had really happened out there. "I hope you don't mind going last but you were not here when I called for line-up."

"Last is good Helen. I really prefer being the last one to be baptized." Jeremiah gave her a handsome smile and waited for her to start sending the group down when he whispered to Cassie. "Being last might be God's plan so I can once again see the past."

"I understand darling. If the Lord should take you back and you are down longer than the others they might start wondering what is holding you down in the water." Cassie tried not to chuckle when she noticed both ministers struggling with pulling an obese man back up from the water. "Poor souls! I cannot tell who had it the hardest just now. The dear man being baptized or the preachers performing his baptism."

"It does make our church baptism by sprinkling water on the head far more-simpler, doesn't it?" Jeremiah could tell Cassie was studying something as her attention was on the constant swirl of the water when a Christian was baptized. "Cassie darling, what is on that beautiful mind of yours?"

"I was observing the water rings as each person was raised up and each time there were exactly two rings." Cassie's eyes locked with Jeremiah's. "Jeremy, I believe if you go before me, I can tell by the number of rings that flow out around you when you rise from the water, if you were visited or not by Jesus. If there are three rings, my guess is you will be. If I go in after you then I may feel where his presence was."

87

"Then I will be happy to go first because the odds of another miracle happening is very likely due to all the other Holy appearances." Jeremy squeezed her hand when one of the baptizing ministers called him forward. "I'll wait out here for you Cassie after I have been raised."

"Thank you darling. I did notice everyone waded out of the river the moment the preachers lifted them up from the water, then turned to witness others being baptize." Cassie gave Jeremiah a little wave, glad he had thought to stay behind so she wouldn't be the last one in the Jordon.

The Ministers gathered on either side of the young preacher and asked him if he were ready to begin. Before Jeremiah could respond, the men doing the baptizing vanished and a rough looking man stood over him, his long unkept hair blowing in the wind. Jeremiah could see this ancient Baptist was dressed in camel hair cloth and his wrist and forearm wore a leather band. A sense of recognition was obvious from both parties as the Baptist spoke.

"Jeremiah, my distant cousin, I was sent to perform the baptism on you in the very spot I was asked by Jesus to baptize him." The young preacher had heard the strong-powerful voice that had called out in the wilderness over 2,000-years ago when he announced to a world in need. "Prepare ye the way of the Lord!" Now, some 2,000-years-later, the same John was prepared to baptize him at the same spot. "Once I take your back in the river and you go under the water of the Jordon, my job here will be done and you shall be greeted by the Lord under the currants of the Jordon."

"It was a pleasure to meet you John and have you to baptize me like you did our Savior." Jeremiah had wondered why he had called him cousin. "I wish we would have had more time to get to know one another."

"We shall have an eternity Jeremiah but for now our time together is slipping past and Jesus awaits below in the water currents for you." John's strong arms held the frail man back as he announced, "I baptized you with the water of redemption." John gently laid Jeremiah down under the water.

Jeremiah could see the swirls in the currents surrounding

him and through a bright light, the face of the Lord appeared. He had a big smile on his face as he drew nearer. "Tonight, after you visit the upper room where my disciples prepared our Passover Meal and where I told them what was going to happen to me, where I handed out the sacraments of bread and wine and asked that they do this often in remembrance of me, then you will take Cassondra and go to the Garden of Gethsemane as the sun is dropping, like I did. There, you shall see glimpses of the past agonies I endured knowing what was lying ahead for me."

"Lord, sense you asked me to take my beloved with me, does this mean she too will witness these glimpses of the past?" Jeremiah suddenly wondered if he actually spoke under water, which is humanly impossible, or was he merely thinking the words and God heard his spirit speaking."

"To answer your first question, yes Cassondra will see this vision for herself for I will be presenting her with her own sacred necklace when she is lowered in the Jordon. Your second question was more like a confuse thought as to how you had just communicated with me while under water. Being human, it is impossible without getting strangled with the water for the lack of breathing. But in my presence Jeremiah, all things are possible." A big smile fell over the Lord's lips. "Now, we shall speak later but our time below must be cut short due to those watching and wondering why you are still down. Jeremiah, you did well to recognize my old foe in the wilderness edge. Lucifer, the ever-present thorn, thought he had you fooled and with his ability to throw his voice made you assume he was just beyond you hidden somewhere in that wilderness. Beware of his clever tricks my brother, because in actuality, Satan was standing just an arm's length away. It is his trick to draw you inside the wilderness and keep calling you as you try to find his location until he gets you lost. Then he leaves you on your own, to search for the way out if you're lucky or simply waste away in the hot-dry desert. My great fallen angel was hoping for the latter to stop you from doing my will."

"Thank you, Lord, for the great advice on how to recognize the devil's tricks and illusions and your servant is more than ready to begin your mission along with Cassie." Jeremiah received a positive nod from the Lord as his head broke free of the water and the young minister could hear the quiet voices on the river bank break their silence like a fortified damn holding back a large body of water, that had just opened up with loud excitement. Their stun silence over counting the minutes the young man was under the water, and assuming no one could hold their breath that long, then watch him rise up in a colorful current sending out three massive ripples, and his cloths radiating in a brilliant light.

As the whispers rose all around him, Jeremiah heard the one voice he knew he could count on, his Cassie. "Jeremy, you must have been having a holy meeting underneath the Jordon's calm water." She glanced around at the many faces watching them. "Everyone watching were getting upset over the minister's refusal to lift you up out of the water and they couldn't understand why I acted so calm and relaxed, even knowing I would be lowered next."

"Cassie, it was amazing down below with Jesus." Jeremiah beamed with happiness. "You know, I think I even asked the Lord a question underneath the water and I never took in one drop of water." He laughed, recalling the words of Jesus. "and, you will never know who actually baptized me and at the very spot Jesus was baptized."

"I would guess, John the Baptist." Cassie gave her own chuckle over Jeremiah's surprised face. "I heard you speaking to him and you called his name out. I am the only one that knew why you said John's name, and no doubt the only one here blessed to hear the Baptist actually speaking and calling you cousin." She gave her fiancé a beautiful smile when the two ministers called her over. "Since I was blessed to see three remarkable ripples in the currant when you came up, I feel certain I shall feel the presence of Jesus lingering below."

"Far better than feeling His presence darling, Jesus Himself will be waiting for you in the flesh and I believe He has something amazing to give you." Jeremiah gave her a kiss and faced her forward. "Now go and be blessed. I shall be waiting for you when you come up."

Cassie glanced back for one last smile before walking between the ministers. After settling into place, she casually asked them. "Gentlemen, I hope you are just as excited over baptizing the last one in line like you are the first to be baptized."

The heavyset preacher glanced over at his partner, knowing they felt the same way over finishing their ordinary day's work but this day was anything but ordinary. "My dear young lady, to be honest, most work days are tiring with all the tourist lined up to be baptized so to reach the last one in line is a relief for us. But, today seems different. It's almost as if the holy one has return to His spot of baptism and seems to favor you and your husband, Reverend Mitchell."

"Reverend Tare, you are correct about miracles happened this day but as for me being Mrs. Jeremiah Mitchell, I must wait a few more hours for that blessed event." Cassie closed her eyes, preparing to be submerged under the water. "I mustn't keep my Lord waiting. Let's get on with it."

As soon as Cassie went under she was looking into the face of the Lord. "Cassondra, I have seen the deep love and affection you feel for my beloved kinsman therefore, I shall grant you the gift of witnessing the things that Jeremiah can see. Instead of wearing a Sacred Cross, you shall have the Sacred Heart necklace, made from the stones of Zion." Jesus spoke soft and clear under the water of the Jordon. "Like Jeremiah, you must wear it out at all times if you are to see what I choose to show you." Jesus had noticed Cassie trying to hold her breath so he asked her "Cassondra, do you love me?" he smiled when she nodded her head, cheeks puffed out, needing to take a breath. "Cassie, if you love me, then tell me. You must have faith Cassie."

Unable to hold her breath she decided to trust the Lord and show her faith. "Yes Jesus, I love you more that everything above this holy river." When she knew she could breathe in the presence of God, she gave a soft laugh. "What a rare feeling Lord to be able to breathed underneath water and sing your praises if I've a mind."

"Just remember sweet sister, do not try this without me

present, understand?" Jesus brought forth an exquisite necklace in the shape of a heart, with stones that sparkled with the colors of the promised rainbow and placed it lovingly around her neck. "Now, I send you up to be with your life-mate. Time is at hand for your visit to the upper room, to break the bread and drink the wine in remembrance of me." With those moving words, Cassie was breaking through the river's service, anxious to tell Jeremy what had happened below and show him her gift from the Lord.

CHAPTER 15

The Upper Room

The couple arrived at the old dwelling that held the sacred Upper Room where Jesus had His last meal with the disciples. Jeremy and Cassie waited patiently out on the street as a group of people were leaving the stone house. They listened to them chatting about the room that was now set up to represent the evening the Lord broke the bread and poured the cup of wine as they made their way down the old narrow street, their tour guide pointing out places of interest.

"I guess they are the last tour group to go though today darling." Cassie smiled up at the man she longed to be her husband. "Maybe there won't be many people touring on their own like us."

Jeremiah took Cassie by her hand and helped her up the uneven steps to the narrow open doorway and noticed the attendant waiting just on the other side. The friendly Jewish man presented a warm smile and his outstretched hand. "Welcome to the wealthy merchant's great home, one might call today, his mansion, due to having two massive floors. The upper floor consisted of one-extra-large room to accommodate the master merchant's grand entertaining and made special by loaning it out to Jesus of Nazareth and his twelve closes followers." The man turned toward a steep staircase made from smooth-cut flat stones and swept his hand dramatically. "Just up that elegant staircase presides the sacred Upper Room. You both came at the perfect time, when the groups with their tour guides speaking and questions are flying around the massive room with high walls that echo back every word, have all left for the day. The constant noise makes hearing the soft voices from the past impossible to hear. When you are alone up there and believe with a pure heart, voices from the past can still be heard as they radiate from the Holy room, that was touched by the hand of God." The man in charge noticed this couple had remained calm and peaceful over his strange proclamation and did not leave in fear. His hopes of locking up early looked bleak. "Forgive me, but, these unusual sounds don't scare you?"

"I find nothing frightening over the heavenly gift of hearing from the past when it involves my Lord and the twelve apostles." Jeremiah glanced up the steep staircase. "I am extremely anxious to climb those stairs and witness once again the things my Lord allows me and Cassie to see. This is the reason we chose this hour to come. Over 2,000-years-ago, Jesus and the twelve would be preparing for their Passover meal around this hour." Jeremiah took out the two passes to get in and laid them in the man's hand, still outstretched. "We are aware the tickets are for nine a.m. till seven p.m. We will not delay your closing sir, for we will leave for Gethsemane directly at seven."

"My dear Mr. Shari, if you are a believer, a Christian Jew, then you might be glad you stayed if you, yourself, listen with a pure heart." Cassie gave him her prettiest smile and walked up the steps behind Jeremiah, leaving the attendant wondering if the things he had been telling people to frighten them away, could actually happen. He made his way quietly up the stairs and set down on the top step to hear for himself if voices from that long ago could actually return in spirit.

The room was almost round and the walls and ceiling faulted up in a high arch. As the couple studied the low reproduction table, similar to furniture in the early AD period and the 13 mix-matched pillows laid out to resemble the famous painting of the Lord's Supper. Cassie spoke softly, not wanting to spoil the moment they might witness what the real Lord's Supper looked like, smelled like.

"I wonder how close the designers of this set are to how it really looked 2,000-years-ago?"

Jeremiah had been listening while at the same time smelling the distinct smell of fire smoke somewhere inside the room. "I believe we shall learn how it looked any second Cassie." He reached for her hand and took it. "The fire I am smelling is coming from the open firepit in the center of the room."

"I smell it darling, as well as something cooking, fried flat bread I believe." Before Jeremy could respond to Cassie, a large pan appeared and smoked with a sweet aroma. "Look, I recognize the man over the cooking pan. It is Andrew, remember on the fishing boat helping his brother Simon Peter with those large nets."

"And look, the table is not setting directly on the floor, it has some kind of risers to accommodate men's outstretched legs and feet beneath the wide cedar table." Cassie watched as a rather stocky disciple stumbled over a stack of large pillows and crashed up against a drying rack, causing a loud crashing noise.

The abrupt noise brought the attendant to his feet, assuming the unusual couple had gotten too close to the Last Supper set and knocked over a costly relic. Prepared for the worse, the usually talkative man was speechless when he noticed the reproduction display was undisturbed and the couple were not even standing near it. They had their attention on something at the other end of the room until he made a gasping sound, then turn to see him peering over the floor at the turned over drying rack.

"Mr. Shari?" Jeremiah placed a finger to his lips, a warning to speak softly as not to disturb the miracle image. "Did you hear the rack falling to the floor" a solemn expression fell across the speechless man. "Mr. Shari sir, you have nothing to fear from being able to hear the past come back to life. It is truly a rare blessing indeed to be able to hear the blessed biblical history come to life and in your case, hear what was said, as Cassie and I can both hear and see things as they really were over 2,000-years-ago." Jeremiah pointed at the overturned drying rack. "The falling drying rack was knocked over by a disciple carrying in a large stack of wood, I imagine to keep the firepit burning while they ate their supper. It was springtime, same as it is now, and the evenings can grow cold after the sun sets."

"How many disciples can you see Reverend Mitchell?" the nervous man spoke softly. "And can they see us?"

"At the moment I count eight men, all busy preparing the

Passover meal as Jesus instructed them. And you need not worry about the twelve witnessing our presence when they all are in attendance." Jeremiah winked at Cassie who couldn't resist hiding her soft laughter over the attendance's humble change. "I can say honestly the man frying the unleavened bread is Andrew, for we witnessed him on the Sea of Galilee struggling with a net filled with fish, a heavenly gift from Jesus." Jeremiah got Cassie's attention and nodded his head toward the man who stumbled over the pillows then knocked over the rack holding a big towel. "I'd say it was Thomas who accidentally hit the rack, knocking it over."

"I agree darling, since I heard Matthew laughed while saying, watch where you're going Thomas. Are you going to get us ran out before we've had our meal with the Lord?" Cassie noticed Mr. Shari had tilted his ear up, trying hard to hear something else. A knock came on the door below and Mr. Shari jumped, obviously thinking someone was at the door below. Before he could respond, he heard heavy feet walking swiftly passed him on the steps and then his eyes flew open when the door below flew open and he heard a loud voice call out.

"It is about time you open this door little James! We have brought the master with us and it is not safe out in the street after dark, what with the high leaders of the church jealous over the attention he has gotten from the people!" Peter motioned for John and brother James to bring Jesus inside.

"Peter, you must not fret so." Jesus smiled at the nervous young man who stood holding the door back. "I shall be safe here, so we can eat this last Passover meal together in peace. There is much I must tell you this night before the time comes for my arrest."

As the disciples walked behind him, stunned in silence as to what he meant, the attendant had been listening to conversation long gone. Although the man could not see the past come to life like the faithful couple, he tearfully felt a sense of humility for this remarkable gift he had been given. So, undisturbed by the modern-outside world, the three loyal Christians listened and Jeremiah, next to Cassie, also witnessed every beautiful word and action that unfolded in the Upper Room over 2,000-years-ago.

As the attendant let the couple out, he could not hold back his tears when they hugged him. Jeremiah gave him a pat on his straight back. "Now you can tell the visitors who come to view the place were Jesus and His twelve had their last supper together, that this holy place does have an echo of their time spent together before they had to scatter from the priest soldiers in the garden of Gethsemane."

"I shall always feel a special bond with you both, for we have shared something that must have been a once in a lifetime occurrence." Mr. Shari gave him his personal card. "If you ever need me for anything, I will always be here to help in what ever mission the good Lord has waiting for you. God bless you both."

Jeremiah left, knowing the Lord had placed this stranger, now a bonded brother of faith, in their life for a purpose, so he stated before leaving. "My brother, I believe the Lord has brought our paths together for the good of His cause, so I know we shall meet again in the very near future. Until then, keep the faith and may the God who has shown the three of us this remarkable blessing, watch over you and keep you safe. Amen."

CHAPTER 16

The Garden of Gethsemane

The sky was showing shades of darkness as Jeremiah and Cassie made it to the hilltop of Gethsemane. They notice several large rocks among the hedges and trees and considered if the garden looked the same as it did when Jesus prayed here while his disciples slumbered near by from an exhausting day. Jeremiah paused at a large stone with a flat service and suddenly felt a chilled breeze blow through the trees overhead. He noticed Cassie watching him and called her over by his side.

"I cannot be certain, but I believe the Lord used this rock to pray his heart out to the Father." The young man's eyes never left the flat stone. "It sits alone here in the grove of trees while the other rocks rest a few yards away." His hand reached down to rub the stone but froze when a light over shadowed the stone and a figure began to emerge. Jeremiah gently pulled Cassie back so they could witness the past again.

Jesus was laying over the flat stone, his hands were trembling violently as he spoke. "Father, please take this cup from me!" the Lord looked upward, a ray of light shining down over Him. "Not my will Father, but Thy will be done. I cannot do as You ask, unless I drink this cup! It is for this purpose that I came into the world! To lay down my life so all who believe might live! Father, give me the strength to carry out your will. For thy will is my will!" then the image of Christ vanished.

"Oh Jeremy, Jesus was tormented and felt great fear, knowing everything he would be going through and the deep amount of pain he must endure." Cassie could not control her own tears.

Jeremiah lowered his hand on the flat stone Jesus had prayed on moments before and he felt a strange sense of power sweep through him as he heard the Lord whisper. "You have just received the strength you will need to carry that cross the full distance when it is your turn. Remember, stay close to the cross and you will see me and watched as my blood flowed down in reach. Then dip your finger in it and even through those watching except for Cassondra, will wonder what you are doing. Touch the finger on your brow and feel the redeeming blood heal you of your illness. You will know what do to when a new friend leads you to the one who will show you the way. Go Jeremiah, and rest now, for tomorrow you will be healed and know your destination."

"Cassie, did you hear the Lord speaking to me?" Jeremiah had been listening carefully and had not seen her reaction to what Jesus was telling him.

"I did hear darling." Jeremiah turned to see her crying. "Tomorrow you will have the strength to carry the cross the last stretch all the way to Golgotha hill and there you will be redeemed by the blood of the Lamb! Praise the Lord!"

"And we shall finally know what the Lord has in place for our mission." Jeremiah thought about the new friend the Lord spoke of. "I wonder if that new friend Jesus said would lead me to our destination will be Mr. Shari?"

"He did seem to place us together darling and what better purpose but to show us the way we are to go." Cassie took Jeremiah arm as he led them back down the path, his trusty flashlight lighting the darken woods.

The Old Part of Jerusalem

Jeremiah and Cassie had paid each place Jesus had been taken after being arrested in Gethsemane as visit, the court of the high priest Caiaphas where they contemned Him of blasphemy against God, the steps of the Roman governor, Pontius Pilate who sent Jesus first to King Herod, who sent Him back to Pilate who could find no fault in the innocent man. As the priest stirred up the crowds to call out to contemn Him, the governor had Jesus flogged, in hopes of satisfying the angry mob. This only wet their appetite for more so Pilate brought out Barabbas, a thief and a murderer and gave them a choice, to release Barabbas, a harden criminal or Jesus, the king of the Jews. The priest stirred the crowd up to ask for Barabbas as they said, we have no king but Caesar! When asked by Pilate what then should be done with this man, Jesus the Christ, your king? Caiaphas along with the priest and the angry mob yelled, Crucify Him!

Now the time had come for the reenactment of the way to Calvary, cross walk. Jeremiah found his place, waiting for the final walk alone on the crowded narrow streets of old Jerusalem. Cassie had found the perfect spot to stand to keep watch over the man she had fallen so deeply in love with. Standing by the edge of the same Roman built stone paved road that Jesus walked over 2,000-years-ago, struggling to carry the very-heavy Roman cross made with solid Dogwood, would help Cassie keep up with Jeremiah as he pulled the same kind of cross. Cassie had offered up many grateful prayers to the Lord for granting Jeremiah the strength he needed to walk the long distance. Nearby she could hear concerns voiced by spectators as they observed the frail man who had signed up for the hardest part of the cross pull. Feeling a comforting hand on her shoulder, Cassie glanced beside her and saw Mr. Shari smiling down.

"I have been sent to give you support and reassure you Jeremiah will do just fine making the hill where he will receive his healing miracle." The comforting words made Cassie relax as she returned his smile. "Now there is that smile that warmed my heart last evening."

"How did you know where to find us Mr. Shari?"

"Cassie, please called me Claude, now that the Lord has brought us together as friends." The tall upper room attendant looked out at Jeremiah when he noticed him watching him speaking with Cassie and threw a hand up in recognition. "Ah, Jeremiah finally remembers where we met." He returned the wave and gave the young man a thumbs-up, then smiled down at Cassie. "To answer your question as to know where I could find you both, I had a visit this morning in the form of a vision and the Lord filled me in on where you would be, what would be happening and what my job would be for helping lead you to Jeremiah's ancestor."

"Jeremiah has an ancestor here in Jerusalem, Claude?" Cassie looked out to give Jeremy an air kiss which he returned, causing their new friend to chuckle softly. "Claude do you find blowing the person you love an air-kiss when they are standing too far to give a real kiss to for good luck, comical?"

"Not in the least Cassie, it is really quite charming. I've just never witness anyone doing it that way before." He glanced out to see the young minister returning Cassie a loving blow-kiss of her own. "I suppose these air-kisses are strictly made for lovers, so I shall stick to giving my young friend a thumb's up."

"That would be more appropriate Claude, now could you tell me about Jeremy's ancestor? Does he live nearby?" Cassie glanced up the street searching for any sign of the person carrying the heavy cross but they had not got in sight yet. She nodded a negative when Jeremiah looked for a signal from her, his view blocked by buildings.

"The relative I speak of does not live in Jerusalem Cassie, but they were in Jerusalem for the Passover Feast as well as the reenactment of the Lord's sacrifice. Due to my friend's long years on earth, he cannot take in all the Holy Weeks festivities, both Jewish and Christian, as he is both."

"Jeremiah just found out recently that he had Jewish kin from his mother's side. Knowing that God first chose the Jewish people for his people and the fact that God's only Son was born a Jew due to Mary's line, as well as His earthly father Joseph's line, both from the house of David, which the prophets foretold, made us both happy to have this blessed bloodline inside his veins. Any child we have will be blessed with the same bloodline."

"Then my dear friend will be overjoyed that both you and Jeremiah are happy with being of Jewish kin and will make taking over the family's special mission a smooth transfer." Hearing the crowds down the street grow louder, Claude and Cassie knew the cross would soon be passed over to Jeremiah. She looked into Jeremy's eyes and no words needed to be spoken as the love that past between them was more than enough. Keeping watch on the man she loved as the tired man carrying the heavy cross managed to pass it over to Jeremiah and she instantly heard the friend next to her pray. "Lord Jesus, keep your servant and brother safe and with the strength of

Sampson to carry your cross up the deadly hill of Golgotha, then bless him with thy redeeming blood. Amen."

"Amen." Cassie whispered softly as she began to walk along beside him on the edge of the narrow way.

Jeremiah could feel the weight of the heavy cross over his thin shoulder and was glad Cassie had not witness what he weighed before leaving the hotel that morning. And even though Jeremiah had dropped to a dangerous 102 pounds at 6'8, he felt strong. He had been too busy taking in the places where Jesus had walked to think about his blood count dropping due to not producing any fresh blood cells and he felt blessed that he had not cut himself from doing even the simples things like shaving. Since he learned about his fatal illness Jeremiah had grown a beard and mustache and he only had to trim it now and shaving became minimal. As he carried the heavy cross down the narrow-curvy streets, his glance would pick up his faithful Cassie, staying right beside him, just a few feet away due to the streets being roped off to the many pilgrims lined up observing the men brave and strong enough to carry such a cumbersome burden the full length.

As Cassie kept up with her beloved Jeremy, she could hear those following and speaking loud enough to hear about the chances of the frail man who was carrying the hardest leg of the cross walk.

"How much longer can the dear man walk without dropping a cross that had to weigh more than he did." One woman seemed passionate over her concern.

"I cannot imagine why the planning committee permitted such a sick man to enter in the reenactment in the first place." One man spoke loud enough to draw Jeremiah's attention, who seem to have more concern for Cassie than he did for himself.

Cassie returned his concern look with a beautiful reassuring smile of her own, to let him know she had full trust in his ability to make it to the hill where he would get the healing miracle they both knew was waiting there. A voice piped up behind her.

"Doris, I know who that fragile young man reminds us of." Two women had been following behind Cassie discussing her fiancé's obvious illness. "Judge Bruster's grandson that had blood disorder and grew so weak he died."

"That's exactly who I was trying to think of Mable! Why, I saw Danny right before he left this world and I swear, he looked exactly like that handsome man baring that heavy cross. Same height as Danny and weighs about the same 100 pounds." She tried to whisper but Cassie could still hear her. "I think that pretty little thing following him is his wife. Poor dear, so young to be a widow."

"Oh, my yes, and to weigh more than your husband cannot feel good." The woman named Mable clicked her tongue and jumped when Cassie turned to face them.

"Ladies, it is obvious you are assuming things that will not happen." They pretended to be innocent when they both repeated

"Who, me?"

"Nice try but I heard everything Mable, you and your friend Doris said. That wonderful man out there carrying that cross down the same Roman road as Jesus did, volunteered to take it up Golgotha Hill. He is my beloved fiancé and he is sick, deathly ill and I can see he weighs around 102 pounds although he is trying to hide that truth from me. At this moment, Reverend Jeremiah Mitchell has got strength to carry that cross straight up that hill better than any strong healthy man here watching. Our great Savior has blessed my Jeremy with all the strength he needs and he shall make it, be made better and carry out the service of our Lord, Jesus Christ." She gave them a positive smile. "Now ladies, perhaps now is a good time to start working on that gossip habit which the Lord-God detest. Excuse me, my wonderful fellow has rounded the curve and is headed up toward the hill." She moved swiftly to catch up leaving Claude Shari to shake his head at the noisy women.

"The church is open until 10:00 p.m. this evening ladies and there is a big fine altar to kneel at for forgiveness prayers." He waved and followed after Cassie as the women stared at one another, jaws dropped.

Golgotha Hill

Jeremiah reached the hill of Calvary and now weary from

the heavy cross, breathed a sigh of relief when two men that had been waiting to finish up the reenactment, took the cross off Jeremiah's back and lifted it over the waiting hole then dropped it in, empty of any tortured soul who had already received great pain from being punished for no crime. Now, the intense agony from the act of crucifixion, would be totally unbearable for the Lamb of God to endure.

Those watching the reenactment were glad they did not have to witness the actual crucifixion of their Savior. Knowing what he had to go through was hard enough without witnessing it. Everyone there could only imagine what the Lord must have looked like at this point, but there were two loyal-faithful children of God who could see just how Jesus looked and sounded, as He moaned with sheer pain when the first nail was driven through His perfect right hand, then the left, and last the feet, one-atop-the-other. Then the moment the cross was lifted and the weight of His beautiful body pulled against the fastened-down nails, the heavy cross fell hard down in the waiting hole, jarring every painful nerve and muscle. His mournful cry tore at the hearts of Jeremiah and Cassie as their tears ran uncontrollably down their face. Some of the people standing dear by them noticed their overwhelming grief and watched them in wonder, as if for some miraculous reason, this man and woman could actually be witnessing the Lord's crucifixion come to life.

Then Jeremiah saw the blood flowing down the cross and suddenly the young minister didn't feel like he had the right to be there to receive this beautiful healing miracle. Seeing everything clearly what the Lord actually went through to save everyone from their sins made the young minister's mind race over everything he had done wrong in his life, including feeling responsible for his father's untimely death. now knowing the Son of God, the only man born of a woman who had never sin and had died in such a painful cruel way, to save him, Jeremiah Mitchell from his sins and to also bless him by healing his fatal disease with His redeeming blood, made him feel unworthy to just reach out and take the sacred blood so he wouldn't suffer and die.

Time was ticking by and the young man grew faint and fell to his knees out of the bloods reach and his sudden movement made Cassie alert to his dilemma. She had been so caught up with watching her Savior crying out His words she hadn't noticed Jeremiah hesitation in taking the blood on his finger as the Lord had instructed him to do. With deep worry and perfect love for this man she had given up everything for, Cassie raced up the hill and knelt down by his side, noticing for the first time how white his skin had turned. With shaky fingers she checked his pulse and got a weak beat and suddenly she felt like she was losing her Jeremy as she lifted him up into her arms and turned his face around to see.

"Jeremy, please darling, you must try to stand up with my help and touch the blood of our Savior before He vanishes!" Cassie could not stop the tears from falling on his face as she watched the man she adored start shaking, then closed his eyes as his arm fell limply under the cross. And just as Cassie thought the life she had thought she would be having with her Jeremy was over, her eyes fell on the drops of blood splatting on his fingers from the cross and looked up expecting to see her Lord dead. Instead, she saw his incredible blue-green-eyes looking down at Jeremiah who had opened his eyes the moment he felt the life-saving blood. All Jeremiah could do was look up into the eyes of his Savior, who, even from the past shadows of his painful death had heard his thoughts about being unworthy to reach up for the saving blood that only he and Cassie could see.

"Jeremiah, you do remember why I gave up my life on that cross for, do you not? Was it not for every sin ever committed, by every person every born? You must learn to forgive yourself my beloved brother so this mission I have prepared for you can be accomplished. It was never your fault that your father was murdered Jeremiah. Lucifer just wanted you to believe it was and that it was justified. My brother, truly, no murder can be judge as justifiable. Our commandment holds true in all cases and THY SHALT NOT KILL is just that! Remember my words, if you even look at a brother or neighbor with hate in your heart, you have committed murder in the sight of God."

In a flash, Jesus stood over Jeremiah and helped him up. "The truth is, my enemy, Lucifer had pretended to be me and he easily killed you father just to keep his soul before you could save him. I know how you struggle with never having the time to save the man who fathered you but you have forgotten that my will and judgement is final and no matter how smart or clever my fallen archangel thinks he is, he can never outsmart the Almighty God. At this moment Satan is confused as to why Harvey Mitchell is out of his reach in the Vale of Siddim, a temporary holding place and protected by my angels down in the pit below the Dead Sea. This is Harvey's resting place until the time is suitable for my judgement weather to make him remain there until I return on Judgement day or bring him up alive and still unsaved, giving him the one chance he had taken away by Lucifer, before you had the chance to help save him."

"Jesus, are you telling me that there might still be a chance to bring my father to you for salvation, if this is your decision?" Jeremiah felt for the first time since he lost both his mama and daddy on his 10th birthday over twenty-years ago, he might still have the chance to help save his daddy's troubled soul. Although the young man could never get his precious mama back and would wait to greet her in heaven someday, he could have another chance with the man who had beaten him and accidentally killed the best thing in his young life.

"Jeremiah, the love I hold for you and Cassondra, I hold for your father, Harvey Mitchell as well. There are reasons why a man changes from a sweet innocent child, who learns about his God and sings the praise songs so lovingly from his small heart and grows up to curse the very God he had loved and revered so much as a sixteen-year-old that he desired to become a minister so he could tell everyone about the One that save him and the world from sin." Jesus knew Jeremiah had never known anything about his father's past, when he too had a heart that burned for the chance to tell everyone the story of Jesus. "You see my brother, your daddy just got lost but he had been changing little by little, unknown to you and your mama Clara. The fire that once burned inside his young soul was rekindled the night he almost killed two-little girls playing near the street." Jesus began to fade away as he made the couple a promise. "Go now with your new friend, the Shari. He will guide you to your kindred where next we meet. There I will let you see for yourself what happened that faithful night that began to change your daddy from following me and what happened just weeks before your tenth birthday that turned his life back around and instantly got Lucifer's attention and why Satan acted so swiftly to take him before he could find salvation with your aid."

Jeremiah and Cassie stared at the empty space were moments before the Lord stood speaking. They had lost all thought of all the spectators watching and listening to just Jeremiah's conversation with someone invisible and silent to them. Before facing the quiet crowd, obviously waiting for some kind of explanation as to what just happened under the empty cross, Jeremiah and Cassie could only look into each other's eyes. They both felt a comforting hand touch their shoulder then watched their tall friend knell down between them.

"While you were conversing with the Lord Jeremiah, I explained things to the spectators and sent them on their way." His smile was warm and pleasant as he stood to assist the couple to their feet. "There is nothing more you need to see here for now. We must leave at once to Nazareth, where your ancient relative lives. He is expecting you and knows of your arrival. There, the Lord will join us to reveal to you everything you shall be doing for Him." Mr. Shari's laugh was magical. "You have been blessed my son, to receive such a powerful mission. It is because the Lord Jesus trust you and your faithful ability that He is granting you and your soon to be wife, this remarkable, once-in-a-life-time opportunity to grant sinners the healing miracle." He looked up to check the position of the sun. "Come, there's no time to waste. We leave at once!"

The group of three were loaded swiftly in Mr. Shari's small car and left the streets of Jerusalem behind them, as the couple wondered what would become of their things left in their honeymoon suite. As they drove away, Jeremiah asked Claude what he had said to the spectators to satisfy their curiosity.

"I simply told them the truth and before they could doubt me, they saw the blood of the lamb drip from the cross on your hand." Claude smiled when Jeremiah opened his hand to find the Savior's blood there.

CHAPTER 17

Nazareth

The car bounced along down the rough road that Claude Shari turned down after reaching the small town of Nazareth. The narrow dirt lane wound its way around one curve after another until an old timber cottage came into view.

"Ah! Finally! There is your relative's very old house." The friendly man chuckled. "It surprises me every time I have the honor to visit it again."

"I guess you do stay busy working all hours being the attendant for the Upper Room." Cassie admired the heavy timber cottage. "What kind of wood is the old house built from Claude? I don't believe I have ever seen any quite like that before." She glanced at Jeremiah and noticed him staring at the well-built cottage. "It is quite stunning isn't it darling? Do you recognize the wood?"

"It had to come from somewhere in Lebanon. That was where Solomon had his big Cedars brought in from when he built the massive temple for God in Jerusalem." Jeremiah had recognized the wood as Cedar, massive Cedar.

"You have a good eye for old wood Jeremiah." Hearing the strong voice next to the car, all three riders turn quickly to see an elderly man with shoulder length white hair and a beard to match, propped up steadily on an old cane. "Welcome to the Jesu Cottage my brother. The cottage was named in honor of my oldest uncle. It is good to finally meet the son of Clara." His face seemed older than his voice and clear-blue-eyes, that had a flicker of sparkle when he smiled. "Alright my lovely family, you may stop staring and climb out from that modern contraption and come inside for a nice glass of wine and an assortment of cheeses and fruit, Memmi's fresh baked bread and her luscious fig-apple cake."

As the polite older gentleman helped Cassie out of the small automobile, she noticed the elegant woman standing by the open door smiling, her thick white hair pulled back and covered with a headdress that resembled something from the bible. "Tell me sir, is that charming lady waiting at the door your Memmi?"

"One in the same, my dear." The jolly man gave Memmi a nod, to make her aware she was the topic of the introductions. From years of experience, the gracious hostess gave them a friendly wave. Cassie return the wave with another obvious question. "Is Memmi your wife Mr. Jesu?"

"That she is my dear, for quite a number of years." The elderly man easily picked up the box Mr. Shari handed him. "Thank you, Claude for picking up my mail. I do not travel down to town as much as I used too." He looked over the group and gave them his crinkle grin. "It is not the saddling up old Lance mind you, that keeps me at home, it riding that stubborn donkey down that dusty-bumpy road for ten miles. It is hard on the old joints."

"So, you don't have a car or truck to make your visit to town quicker and easier sir?" Jeremiah followed behind his unusual relative, who seemed to know his dear mother.

Young Jeremiah, when I grew up we did not have any thing that required gas, which also came years later. The only other thing we had to carry us to and throw, besides a reliable donkey, mule, or horse, if one was rich, was a wooden cart with two large wooden wheels." A far away look fell on the gentle face.

"I can still hear my dear-departed father telling my beloved saintly mother that he had just built her the finest cart in all of Nazareth." He grew melancholy as his eyes grew misty. "My-my, has it been that long ago? Yet, I can still see them so clearly. Older in years but still very much in love with one another."

"Simon dearest, must you carry on so." The wife was quick to come to his rescue. "You know, as well as I, that one day soon we shall see the family again and have a big reunion." She took his hand and they shared a smile before she turned to their guest. "You must not let Simon's beautiful remembrance of our loving family disturb your visit with us. We have been waiting for such a long time to join our blessed family in heaven and now that you are here Jeremiah, our special kin we have been expecting ever since you were born, we are so overwhelmed with joy and excitement at your arrival we both feel a bit giddy, that is all."

"Then, you have been waiting for me to come here and take over this mission Jesus asked me to do for Him?" Jeremiah stopped at the old narrow doorway and wrapped his arm around Cassie's waist. "If you don't mind my asking, but how did you learn about me, living far away from you in the coastal town of Marsh Cove, North Carolina, U.S.A.?"

"You precious mother wrote us the minute you were born, Jeremiah." Memmi took his hand. "Clara Marie was from the house of James, the descendent we have been in search of from the son of James, Jeremiah Jesu Joseph Mitchell"

"Jeremiah, it is time for you to know who your descendance were and why it was important for you to take over the family's life-long mission to preserve the reminiscence of the blood shed by Jesus, our brother." Simon regained his composure and led the group inside the large old cottage. "This very old home was built by our amazing father over 2,000-years-ago and it is the only dwelling from the time of Jesus that is left standing. Jeremiah, can you guess the reason why this old home still stands after so many years have past since it was first built for my father's young bride?"

"I believe I can tell you the reason, Uncle Simon." Jeremiah felt strange knowing what he was about to share with the woman he was hoping to marry soon. "The reason it stands is not because it had the very best carpenter in its day, it was due to the one special Son that lived here, within these standing walls." His eyes were on Cassie when he spoke and he noticed her eyes light up as excitement escape her perfect lips.

"Jesus lived here and Joseph built " her eyes wandered around the large room as she tried to visualize the Holy Family living here, happy together as one big family. "if Jesus touched it, then that makes it immortal!" Cassie laughed and hugged Jeremiah. "Darling, you are from the family of Mary and Joseph!" she paused, looking serious. "Jeremy, it had to be obvious to your mama that she was from this holy family, so why didn't she ever tell you of something so incredible?"

"Perhaps mama was waiting until I grew older and had time to build my faith in the belief that Jesus Christ was indeed the Son of God and our blessed Savior who had given up His earthly life to save us all." Jeremiah had thought back to his mother's faith-walk and recalled the amount of spiritual and material sacrifices she had made for him and his bad-tempered father. "I guess she was about to share that sacred part of our family heritage when she said we had a trace of Jewish blood in us." Jeremiah's memory of that evening when his mama opened up about her lost relatives flooded back into his mind.

"It is all coming back to me now. I was seven-days-away from my 10th birthday and mama said she had something very important to share with me. Something amazing that would change my life forever when I returned to her homeland. I still can hear her soft words, knowing daddy might hear this wonderful news she was about to share with me."

A Little Over Twenty-Years Ago

"Son, you and I are of Jewish kin and our special family, far away in Israel, will present you with a glorious honor, which, up until now, has only been held from the male side of Simon, the son of Mary. My Jewish father, Rabi Jeremiah Joseph, was the last son and he had only one child, a daughter, me. Uncle Simon considered giving father the honored mission but knew the time wasn't right, so that would wait for Jeremiah Senior to have a son of his own. Since that was not to be, they would except his grandson, which is you Jeremiah darling."

"Clara! Do you insist in filling that boy's mind with your stupid-religious garb!" Harvey appeared from the shadow of the doorway. "I'll have no more talk about your marked past Clara! To admit you are a Jew out on the streets of Marsh Cove could get all of us killed! You know half this town detest any Jews setting down roots here much less opening a business!"

"Half of my family are Jews Harvey and the house of Joseph should always be respected over all other houses! "Jeremiah remembered how his usually frail mother spoke up unafraid, to defend the one perfect thing she had inherited from her poor father. "Our family might have been poor in wealth

Harvey Mitchell, but the head of the house of Joseph could boost of one thing no other family on earth could ever claim. The Son born of his wife Mary was "

"Clara, I warned you to never mention that name in my house again!" Jeremiah recalled how angry his father had grown over her beautiful words and the sound of his loud slap across her mouth that caused her to lose her balance and fall hard on the floor still radiated in the young pastor's head. "I was stupid to believe in Him in the first-place woman!" Harvey picked up a large log for the fireplace and shook it. "He is about as real as those dying embers inside this firebox, you were about to let burn out while making up a crock of lies to appease this no-account young'un you've raised! Your great worthless kin have done nothing to help get us out of poverty!" he laughed out. "If this wonderful son is so amazing, why can't he rain down millions upon his poor-helpless family?"

"You have no heart Harvey, to speak ill of our Lord." Jeremiah remembered how his mother had stood her ground with her fallen husband, the man she had once loved and believed in. "You cannot blame God for your bad choices Harvey, and although you have sunken about as low as you can go, one plea to the Lord for forgiveness can easily turned you back around to good."

Harvey grabbed a hand full of money from the jar where Clara had put the bill money. "I will not stand around here listening to your pathetic sermons woman!" Harvey narrowed his eyes at Jeremiah. "I'm your father kid so I am telling you to stop listening to your wicked mother's lies about this person that has never existed!" Harvey Mitchell stormed out the door, leaving Jeremiah's mother in tears.

"Jeremiah, I think it is time you know why your father became the cruel man you remember and blame yourself for his unsaved salvation." Jesus had broken through the dense fog of his past memories with his parents and the Lord needed Jeremiah to be healed from his childhood trauma so He could prepare him for a higher calling to help save the lost and hurting through the redeeming blood of the Lamb.

113

CHAPTER 18

Marion, North Carolina: 1956

"Graduates of the 1956 class of Marion High School, it is my honor to introduce for the commencement speaker, Reverend Billy Graham." The students and parents stood clapping for the well-known evangelist. A young man seated near the front could not hide his tears over the special speaker he had admired ever since his grandparents took him to see Doctor Graham when he was ten. It was the first tent revival young Harvey Michell had ever been to and he knew he could never share the special-one-week experience with his atheist parents, but he was bursting to share his moving experience with his two best friends, Toby and Daniel. The three friends share the same belief in God, the Creator of all things, but each friend believed different kinds of religion. Toby was a strong Catholic, Daniel was a Jew and Harvey grew to believe from his grandma and grandpa Mitchell's Baptist faith. But, their love and dedication for one another made them strong in their friendship.

Everyone listened to the moving speech where Reverend Graham spoke of the hope to succeed in the world where people continue to struggle with things of this world with no thought of their Holy Creator who alone made everything they see, feel and touch. "You may find yourself reaching for the stars, the highest paid job out there, a seat in government or the highest seat a person can achieve, President of the United States, But, not one of these earthly things can give you the hope you've been seeking. Life will go on and your search for that gift of happiness might seem like it is in reach until you claim the thing you were after, but it too grows cold while you grow older." The powerful preacher lifted high his bible. "Young ones, your life is in front of you and the journey through this life brings with it challenges. You find yourself making decisions, whether to go left or right, you set your goals high. Maybe a doctor, a lawyer, a soldier, a general, a nurse or teacher, but without real hope in your heart when you come full circle, your children grown with children of their own, do you still hold the special hope I speak of in your heart? There is only one source of the hope I speak about and that is the hope that will continue on after this life is over. My young friends, Jesus Christ is that hope I speak of. As you busy yourself with the things of this world and lose track of our Blessed One, He is always there, outside your heart, knocking, waiting for you to open your heart back up to Him and find your gift of hope still there, tucked safely away. Hopefully all of you will have a long life ahead and find love and joy in all areas of your life, but life on this earth is like a fleeting wind and as you busy your life away, before you know it you realize it's almost over and you wonder were the years went. This is where hope takes over. Jesus said, I am the way, the truth and the life, no-one comes to the Father, but by me. See my young friends, live your beautiful life the Lord gave you here on earth without fear of tomorrow, for we all simply leave this old world behind and go to a far better place where that peaceful hope will take you on the wings of a heavenly angel."

Harvey Mitchell left the football field with the love pf Jesus burning in his heart and he knew, without a doubt that he wanted to be a preacher like Billy Graham and tell the world about the Lord's salvation.

The Mitchell Home

"Harvey, who was the commencement speaker this year?" Bertha Mitchell set the table and checked the hall clock for the time, knowing Calvin would be home from work soon. "Was it the governor again? God, I hope not! That man can give one boring speech."

"No mama, it wasn't the governor." Harvey knew trouble would hit the fan when he told his parents who gave their class the graduation speech. "Principal Patterson let the students choose who we wanted to speak this year, so it was unanimous."

"Unanimous?" Calvin Mitchell had walked inside just in

time to hear their conversation. "Who could be so popular that the entire class voted on them?"

"Reverend Billy Graham, that's who." Harvey had been built up by America's most respected Christian leader and he felt the strong power of God overtake him.

"Billy Graham, that revival preacher my folks brag about?" Calvin narrowed his eyes at his son. "Alright boy, tell me the damn truth! You said the vote was unanimous, so does that mean, you voted on that man too?"

"The word unanimous means 'everyone agreed' doesn't it, father." Harvey knew he had to take up for his faith or be considered a hypocrite, so this time he would not remain still. "Yes father, I voted yes with my fellow students."

"Calvin, our Harvey didn't wish to be singled out as the only student holding out after his entire class voted for this fraud teacher." Bertha reached over to pat her son on his cheek. "Isn't that right son?"

"No mother, that is nowhere near right." Harvey stood tall. "When his name was suggested, I was the first to hold my hand up high!"

"Then who was the person responsible for bringing up this story-tellers name in the first place?" Calvin Mitchell grew irate "I will see that he or she will never receive an invitation to Raven Hill College if they should apply for an entry!"

"Then that suits me just fine father, because being the one that suggested Reverend Billy Graham to my student body, I have been excepted at Duke University where I will finish four-years of college before entering the divinity school there." Harvey knew they would never pay for his college now but he did not need their help after receiving a full scalar ship from Duke with his excellent grades and the desire to become a minister of the Methodist faith.

"You have gone behind your mother and my backs, knowing exactly how we both feel about this so-call religious nonsense and you stand here bragging about THE COLLEGE YOU DECIDED TO ATTEND!" he yelled. "Just pack your things Harvey and get the hell out of our lives!"

"Calvin, where would our son go if we send him away?"

Bertha felt some motherly emotions but Calvin was angry over his son's choice.

"We do not have a son anymore Bertha!" His eyes burned down on his son. "As far as I am concern, you can rot in hell! I never want to see your face again!"

"Isn't it funny sir, a man who doesn't believe in God believes in this Hell where Satan takes the lost souls!" Harvey knew he would be welcomed at his grandparents, but he knew he would never stop praying for his mother and father's lost souls. "Even though you have disowned me, I shall never stop praying for your salvation!" Harvey raced up the steps, packed a few favorite things, and went out the window, not wishing to let his father get the last word or have his sad mother see him leaving.

Present Time: Nazareth

"You are right Lord, father was burning with the desire to preach your gospel when he was a youth, yet something changed in his life to make him behave just like the father he fought to be loyal to his newfound faith." Jeremiah had never seen his father in that light before and he needed to know what happened to change him completely."

"Let me pick up Harvey's story as he was about to start his last year at Duke Divinity School. Studying had kept the young man too busy to do much after school activities, like going out with his friends or dating girls. That all changed when his friend Daniel had a visit from his first cousin. A very beautiful Jewish girl from Israel, whose bright personality had caught the attention of almost every boy on campus. Harvey was no exception and being best friends with Daniel made getting setup on their first date a simple task for the young matchmaker. Daniel had hoped that his good friend Harvey would get his cousin's attention so the three friends could now all have a special woman in his life. So, Harvey and Clara made up the third couple for all their free time.

Halfway through the year, Daniel decided his girl wasn't the woman he wanted to be his life's mate, so he dumped Gail for Stacy Blackwood, a glamorous model from New York City.

117

When the couples met for drinks in the Tavern on Campus, Clara and Ronda started feeling unconvertable with Daniel's flirty date. The men never seem to let Stacy's aggravating habits bother them, but Clara and Ronda sat quietly listening to the rude jokes, Stacy's popping her chewing gum, the high-pitch nasal laughter that would follow every vulgar wisecrack she made about other men and woman seated nearby them.

"Clara, I just cannot for the life of me figure out what those men of ours sees in that New York trash." Ronda whispered, but knew their boyfriends were not interested in what they were saying.

"Well, since all three of those charming men are attending divinity school, I think we are safe to think they won't all desire the cheap she-devil if she tries to lure them to her bed." Clara had remained a virgin and was saving herself for the man she would marry, and she had hopes it would be Harvey, Clara had found herself madly in love with the tall-raven-hair southerner from North Carolina.

"Clara, I just cannot understand why your intelligent cousin picked that bimbo in the first place over our swell friend Gail." Ronda watched the flirty blonde take out something that resembled a cigar and lit it, then noticed the bartender stop to sniff the air, and she quickly mashed it out and replaced it back inside its case before picking up her wine glass just as the bartender made his rounds around the room. "Clara, did you see what just happened over by our guys?"

Clara glanced up, where she had been studying her lessons and noticed the bartender stopping at their table where the men huddled around the enchanting model. "Did something happen to bring the bartender around?"

"I think something almost happened until the quick Bartender caught a whiff of smoke in his tavern." Ronda nodded toward the innocent looking blonde, easily charming the unknowing worker. "I just hope that man doesn't come over here and asked us if we saw anyone lighting a joint."

"Good Lord Ronda, is that what you saw?" Clara punched her friend when she noticed the bartender making his way to their corner. "Ronda, be careful if you are asked anything. You know God detest lairs." Clara added between her teeth. "Just let me do the speaking. We are being observed by that blonde and our fellows. I do believe if we were to say anything negative against that big flirt, they would get mad at us for squealing."

Ronda nodded a positive and picked up her wine before giving the man her prettiest smile.

"Ladies, I do not wish to bother you on your night out, but I was wondering if either of you charming ladies happen to see anyone in here smoking pot?"

"Smoking pot?" Clara gave an innocent look. "I have not been here for very long Mr. Craver, but what few times I have been inside this quant tavern I have never noticed anyone doing drugs. I did smell smoke for a brief moment when I was studying my lessons for tomorrow's college test, but at the time I smelled it I thought someone had lit their table candle." An honest answer due to thinking that very thing when she smelt smoke. "If I see anything suspicious, I will let you know."

"You madam, are a gracious lady." His attention went to the three men huddled around the blonde. "Do except my apologies if I am being too personal, but are two of those young gentlemen your dates by any chance?"

"Yes sir, the two on either end of their good friend Daniel and his new girlfriend." Clara looked over to see them all laughing again. "The New York native seems to be the life of the party, at least to the men folk."

"I can see that and I really do not understand why those fellows of yours are up there with that party girl instead of being back here with their own beautiful, smart and true charming ladies." The owner and bartender noticed their wine and recognized it as their cheapish. "I see you are both having the Davenport red wine, reasonably priced and taste fairly good." He glanced up at the girl who had the boy's attention and noticed she was enjoying a glass of La'Parria, a prices French wine. "Ladies, I am almost certain the young lady entertaining your men started to smoke pot and I would go on to believe she might be a classy drug dealer by her clothes and choice of beverage. Maybe it might be a good time to have your dates come back to be with the better ladies they brought.

Clara smiled and glanced over to see Harvey finally observing her, along with Toby, getting the attention from the handsome owner who had come back with four fresh glasses and a fancy bottle of French wine. Stacy noticed she had lost Harvey and Toby's attention and twirled around to see what had her audience's attention. Her long fingers reached for each boy's arm.

"My adorable friends, you had better race over there before that bartender opens that very expensive bottle of wine your girlfriends ordered or you might find yourselves back in the kitchen washing dirty glasses for a month here." The flirty blonde lifted up her class of the same wine. "I guess the poor darlings think one of you lovely gentleman offered to buy me this wine, never knowing I had the money to set the four of us up with a drink." She batted her long eyelashes at Harvey. "Poor dear, I can recognize an envious woman when I see one."

"Who? Clara, envious?" Harvey politely slid back his chair, thinking to himself 'And little lady, I can read a big flirt when she is around.' "If you will excuse me Daniel, I need to get back to my charming Clara, who I can trust never asked for the high-price wine in the first place." He gave Daniel's new girl a smile. "It was nice meeting you Stacy. You have yourself a great guy here so keep all your flattering remarks for him." He pulled his other friend's chair back. "Come along Toby, I think we have been away, from our babes far, too long."

Clara smiled up at Harvey's and held up a waiting glass for him. "Harvey, you and Toby must be mind-readers. Our very charming host Cliff, presented us with their best wine for being honest and polite." She continued to smile as Harvey looked perplexed over at his friend Toby as they took their seats. "The delightful owner of the tavern asked us if we saw anyone lighting up pot, so I told him the truth." Clara tried hard not to laugh as she watched the blood drain from their shocked faces. "My goodness Harvey darling, you and Toby suddenly look so pale. You wouldn't know who was doing drugs by any chance, would you? The smoke I smelled did come from the area you four were seated at."

"Then, you just smelled some smoke briefly and assumed right away it was pot?" Harvey gave a shaky smile. "This tavern has table candles Clara, so you probably smelled candle smoke."

"And that is exactly what I told that lovely man Cliff I assumed it was, since my head was down looking over my lessons for tomorrow's classes.

Harvey and Toby let out a relief breath as Harvey commenced to pouring the rich wine. "Then that was the honest truth you where speaking about." He took a sip of the excellent wine. "Mumm, and I say honesty pays off. This wine is the very best I have ever had."

"Just admitting that I did smelled smoke gave me the high marks." She exchanged looks with her friend Ronda, watching their dates take a big gulp. "The very clever bartender said he knew right away there was smoke and that some drug pusher was lighting up a joint." The girls hid their giggles when their dates got strangled over her announcement. "He said he could recognized that smell anywhere as well as which table it was coming from."

"And it's a good thing that nice man didn't ask me if I saw anything suspicious." Ronda easily took a drink of the wine. "All I can say is, you fellows better be careful who you hang out with. Daniel's new girl has a wild steak inside her and she just might get you fellows in some serious hot water."

"You saw her light that short smoke?" Toby swallowed, hoping no one had caught them with her.

"Harvey, maybe you ought to warn Daniel about his new girl's bad habits before she gets him in serious trouble with the law or worse still, killed."

"If I do, Daniel might tell me to mind my own business and get lost." Harvey stared down in the red wine, afraid of losing his great friendship with Daniel.

"Sweetheart, sometimes to save the ones we love we must try to save them from themselves. "If it makes things better for you, I will go with you when you speak to him. Take Toby if you had rather but do it when Stacy is no where around. I've notice how she can put on an act and fool the smartness man alive."

Joan Byrd

"Except me, my dear Clara." Cliff Brenner, the owner and bartender had been listening. "Harvey, you and Toby better stay away from that gal, and if it's possible talk some sense into that young friend of yours. I've seen my share of girls like that fellows, and I can tell you true, that one is dangerous."

CHAPTER 19

Back to the Present: Nazareth

"Neither Harvey or Toby could persuade their friend Daniel that his new willing partner was wrong for him, time crept forward with only three more weeks left until graduation. After a few months of silence for his friends, Daniel finally showed up at Harvey's dorm room, completely wasted on drugs. His clothes were dirty and torn, his manner had changed from the decent young man they knew to a complete bum. Harvey could only stare down at the shell of the young man he had known and loved and the only thing that could escape his lips was his name.

"Daniel?"

"Please Harvey, you must help me! I need a fix man!" the once bright young man cried out. "I need a hit badly!"

"Daniel, did that New York blonde turn you into a drug addict?" Harvey helped his old friend inside and after looking around in the hallway for any observers and not seeing any, shut the door and led the upset man to the sofa. "Daniel, you are a sick man buddy. I need to call the hospital and see if they can take you in for rehab and clean you out."

"I just need a fix man, can't you see!" Daniel held up his hands, shaking uncontrollably. "Just loan me a few hundred dollars man so I can buy some weed!"

"I can see you need help Daniel because you are a sick man and if you keep putting that poison inside you it will kill you!" Harvey felt sharp pity for the young man he had always admired and looked up to, and to see him ruined with drugs cut the religious young man badly. "I'll help you Daniel."

A shaky smile fell over the pale face as he tried to slap Harvey's back thankfully. "I'll not buy another drop of drugs from that cheap little whore Stacy. We can get the good-clear smack at Mr. Wise's Crack House, down on East Randle Street."

"East Randle? Daniel, are you serious? That east side is known for corruption and Mafia type organizations! Those people will kill you over a few dollars left unpaid!" Harvey took his hand and the irate young man jerked it back. "I only want to help you get better Daniel! You will die if we don't get you help now. Let me help you get better dear friend."

"Damn your empty words! As far as I am concern, you are no friend of mine Harvey Mitchell!" Daniel stumbled to the door and Harvey tried to stop him. "Take you hands off if me you bastard! I can get drugs on my own! Why I came to you in the first place I'll never know!"

"You came so I could help you Daniel! If you go out that door for more drugs, they could finish you off this time! Is that what you want Daniel? Do you want to die?" by now Harvey was in tears, scared for his friend. "Please, let me help you."

"Keep your no-count help Harvey! From now on you are no friend of mine!" he slung the door open. "Do not try to stop me, I will find someone who will help me!"

"Daniel left angry that night and that was the last time Harvey saw his best friend awake." Jesus had been telling Jeremiah and Cassie about the young minister's father. "He had been begging Clara to marry him and after his grades dropped due to his need of her, she excepted and the young couple were wed in Duke Chapel two months before graduation. Life seemed a lot better with Clara by his side, so the young man built his grades back up and was sure to graduate with the rest of his classmates. Things were looking up for the couple when Harvey received his first church charge. The Mason Hills Methodist Church had 500 active members and another 200 inactive members on the role. The ambitious young minister had high hopes of reinstating most of the non-active members to fill up the empty pews on Sundays. Harvey and Clara had made a trip up to Mason, North Carolina to check out the church and it was while they were there, word came about Daniel's serious accident. They rushed to the hospital and found his mangled body strapped up to monitors and in a coma. The doctors didn't give Daniel long to live due to the drug effects on his brain making the healing senses none responsive to the medications he had been given.

Harvey made visits to sat with his friend along with Toby, his other friend, who could only recall their happy times together. Each friend would speak to the comatose young man, in hopes of a miracle but none came. Harvey prayed for hours on behalf of his fallen friend that we, the Father, myself and the Holy spirit, would forgive Daniel for being weak and unable to get off the thing that was destroying him. One visit made Harvey's life change forever and the sad thing was, the bright young man who burned with fire for the church, fell into the same temptation as his friend Daniel and sank into the man you remember."

"Stacy showed up at the hospital?" Jeremiah had felt some hope for his abusive father until his life was altered by a fallen woman with an agenda. "I guess she must have put on a perfect act for my father to fall for her story?"

"Stacy is well rehearsed in lying and she seems to always fool her victim into her trap. Dressed in a white turtleneck sweater and a black long skirt, the pretty blonde walked quietly into Daniel's room. Without speaking to the handsome man seated next to her ex-boyfriend, Stacy moved over to the other side of the hospital bed and pulled out a tissue to catch the falling tears. She whispered close to the unconscious man's ear that she was so sorry this had to happen to such a wonderful man that she cared so deeply for. Then, without looking at the one she really came to see, she pretended to speak to Daniel."

Duke Hospital: Room 3-A

"Daniel darling, I'm sorry if I made you believe I didn't love you because I refused to buy you more drugs." She wiped her eyes. "I said that because I did love you and I could see how those horrible drugs you got hooked on was destroying you. Daniel, I just wanted to protect you from that evil Max Marvel. I begged you not to go there darling. Those drug dealers on East Randle are deadly and I tried to warn you how they slip a mickey inside the drug's powder when they know you cannot pay. They make it appear like you had an overdose when in fact they put enough toxic drugs inside that one pack to fry your beautiful brain." Stacy was now weeping uncontrollably. "Daniel, my beloved Daniel, why didn't you listen to my warning?" her head fell down on his chest as she whelped.

Moved by her acting, Harvey got up to comfort her, thinking her safe. "There, there Stacy, you must not blame yourself for Daniel's choices. I have put in so many prayers for my friend even if he doesn't get that miracle I hope for, I feel sure that our loving Lord will forgive his sins and except him into his eternal kingdom."

"Oh Harvey, you are such a good man." Stacy looked up, sincerity written on her face. "Clara is a lucky girl to have you for a husband."

"I am the lucky one, believe me Stacy. Clara is the very best thing that has ever happened in my life."

"Clara is the perfect lady for you Harvey and I wish only the best for you both." Stacy straightened up her shoulder bag strap. "I have decided to go back home to New York and start afresh. There's nothing left for me here. Daniel is all but dead and I need to put my life with him behind me."

"But, how can you just walk away when Daniel is still alive, still breathing?" Harvey stepped back when she glanced down at Daniel's peaceful face.

"Harvey, I have faced the sad truth about this man we both love. Daniel is same as dead now darling, and all the prayers you send up to this God of yours won't help that empty body lying there get that miracle you hope for." Stacy moved over and laid her soft hand on Harvey's hand. "Forgive me for what I am about to say, but I don't have the same faith as you do. I am an unbeliever in this so-call God but I still feel the same pain you do, the same heartbreak you do, and" her eyes met his "The same feelings of love and the need to make love with the right man." She broke away and moved over to gently rubbed the face of Daniel, then his silent lips. "I shall never again feel these lips over mine or feel the passion we once had almost every night, until the wee hours of the morning." Once again, she brought on the tears. "This is why I must leave. This, and the one fact I cannot never share with the real man I have always desired and loved the most." She glanced over sadly. "You see darling, the man I love is happily married and getting ready to move, then start a new-faith-feeling career."

"Then it truly is best if you leave for New York Stacy, the sooner the better." Harvey felt sure she was speaking about him. "To even dream about making love to a married man is considered adultery in the eyes of God."

"This is why I leave today." Stacy reached in her bag and pulled out a folded piece of paper. "My one-way ticket to home."

"Then I shall be saying goodbye Stacy and I hope and pray you find happiness but mostly, find your way to the Lord Jesus, so we can meet again one day in heaven." Harvey started putting on his jacket as Stacy walked slowly to the door and turned slowly. "Harvey, do you have classes this afternoon?"

"I have the day off due to our finals starting tomorrow. I'm heading home to crack open the books and study while Clara is taking her last two classes." Harvey moved back next to his silent friend. "Daniel, I will come back tomorrow after exams are finished, so don't start playing checkers without me." An inside joke between the fellows. He reached down and rubbed his cold hand. "I miss you buddy." Feeling teary eyed himself, Harvey walked out in the hallway and button up his jacket. "Are you headed for the airport now Stacy?"

"I still got a few more things to pack and I guess I'll call a cab, since the man next door is at work. He was going to take me, so he could help with my heavy luggage that has to be brought down two flights of steps." She shook her head when they stepped on the hospital elevator. "I don't know how I will manage by myself." she gave a soft laugh. "I cannot expect the cab driver to offer his help without needing a big tip and I'm almost out of cash."

"If you can be ready in thirty-minutes or less, I would be happy to give you a hand with the luggage and drive you down to the airport, but, I only can spare one hour." Harvey knew to do a kindness was always a blessing. "One hour?"

"One hour is perfect Harvey and I promise to hurry with packing that last bag." She gave a big smile. "This is perfect. I will get to the airport in plenty of time without rushing!" she gave him a tight hug, pressing her large breast up against his chest. "You are a dear friend and I am lucky to have had you in my life." She followed the unsuspecting would-be preacher to the parking lot. Knowing her well-laid-out plan had worked so far. Now all she needed was to get him warm and relaxed with a glass of wine, then up to her bedroom where her would be luggage wasn't waiting, just her sexy lustful body waiting to turn him on.

Present Time

"Did that tempting trash get what she was after?" Jeremiah had seen the best of his father and now he felt sure he was about to witness his downfall.

Harvey and Clara hadn't been married for only one month after Daniel showed up at Harvey's dorm room and she never thought anything about her new husband wanting to go sit with his comatose friend after hearing about his accident. Harvey had proved a wonderful lover and she had enjoyed their intimate time together, but with their classes staring early and finals coming up, Clara had to politely asked her very passionate husband to wait until the weekend.

For Harvey, waiting was difficult, but spending his spare time at the hospital when Clara was still having classes, made it easier on his sexual cravings. When Toby asked him one day at the hospital how his married life was going, Harvey told him how much he had enjoyed making love to the woman he loved but college made it difficult to find time for bedroom fun. Unknowing by the two friends, they were not alone. Ease-dropping from the small opening in the doorway, Daniel's ex Stacy enjoyed what she heard from the handsome soon-to-be preacher and she wanted some action with the stud.

Friday finally came around and Clara had morning classes, then she would be free for the weekend, except getting in a few hours to study for the finals which would be given starting Monday. Harvey had finished his classes and except for studying a few subjects, he was completely free for the rest of the weekend. He walked inside their bedroom having his second cup of coffee and took his front row seat on the side of the full-size bed, still unmade. Harvey's eyes fell hungrily down his wife's shapely body when she stepped from the bathroom with just a towel around her. Clara blew him a kiss before pulling out her underwear. She faced the mirror and dropped the towel causing her husband to grow in passion. He had been suffering all week and now he was at his breaking point and he needed to have Clara now. Harvey set the cup down and made his way over as she was preparing to snap up her bra and stopped her. His hands covered her breast as he bent over to kiss her smooth tan neck. Needing her husband too but knowing they just didn't have time, Clara reached for his hands and gently pulled away. After a lot of convincing that he could have all the time they needed when she returned at lunchtime, he reluctantly stepped aside. So, Clara went to classes and Harvey went to sat with his silent friend, until Stacy showed up, knowing by Friday, her catch would be easy to turn on and would not be able to stop once they got started.

CHAPTER 20

Stacy's Penthouse Apartment

Harvey still had not suspected Stacy of lying about leaving when they pulled up in front of a ritzy townhouse. Thinking it was a duplex apartment instead of a single dwelling, the happily married man climbed from the car and got out to open the door for who he thought had become a lady. Her smile was innocent enough when she escorted him up the steps to the front door and unlocked it.

"Come on in and make yourself at home. I'm afraid I can't offer you any tea or coffee. I packed it up and carried it over to my next-door neighbor Margie Mason, a widow woman who lives on just her social security." She looked inside the refrigerator and sighed. "Oh darn, I forgot all about opening that expensive wine last night. Margie don't drink and I hate the thought of pouring it down the drain. My landlord said to clean everything out before I left for New York." She snapped her fingers and walked over to a packed box and retrieved two wrapped up wine glasses. "We have a few minutes, why don't we have a toast for old friend sake and our beloved Daniel." Once again, Stacy brought on the tears. "Daniel loved this wine the best of all. That's why I bought a bottle last night, to pour me a glass and stepped out on the patio and gaze up at the stars, just like we use too before he got sick."

"I'll take a half glass full Stacy. I really need to get home and start studying in for my finals so I can graduate with my Clara." He was glad to see her smile and turn to pour him just the half glass he asked for.

"Here you go friend." She lifted her glass. "A toast, to the two people we love, Daniel and Clara." As he smiled and began drinking the wine, she knew he would be feeling the added surprise she had put in the glass earlier within minutes, so she excused herself to go finish packing, telling the unsuspecting gentleman to enjoy the wine and she would call when to come up to get the bigger suitcase.

Finishing the wine, Harvey set the wine glass down and suddenly grew warm around his privets He suddenly wished he could leave for home but he had promised Stacy he would help her with her luggage and drive her to the airport. He walked to the front door for some fresh air to clear his head. "I need to leave! I need Clara!" he glanced back into the house when he heard Stacy call. "Oh Lord, what can I do?"

From a soft male voice, he heard "Call her a taxi and go home to your wife."

Harvey paused and looked around at the empty porch, the empty parking lot. His brow creased as he stated to himself "Who said that?"

"Harvey, you asked me what you should do about your need for Clara. The answer is, go to her and leave this fallen woman's home quickly before you sin against your beloved wife as well as your God." The voice of Jesus answered, next to Jeremiah and Cassie.

Jeremiah could tell his father was confused by the unseen voice so hoping not to upset Harvey more Jeremiah spoke up, to see if his voice could be heard as well. "Listen to your Lord Harvey and depart from this evil woman who has set you up just as she did your best friend Daniel."

"Two voices speak a warning." Once again Harvey heard Stacy call down, this time louder. "My heart tells me to listen to your warnings. She did trick me, by pretending she lived in duplex and this is a single house, with furniture. Now that I think about it, the refrigerator had other items inside and she was supposed to have everything out. Another lie, obviously."

"You are my brother Harvey, and I am your Lord, who loves you and watched you suffer what you almost done just now." Jesus soft calming voice overrode the loud call of Stacy's voice. "In your previous life, you did go up and wound up a drug-boozing loser that beat your wife Clara as well as your little son."

"You are telling me that this has happened before and the first time I messed up and fell for Stacy's act!" Harvey couldn't control his tears. "And I would hit the beautiful girl I gave my

Joan Byrd

heart to and the son we had?"

Harvey thought about the previous words. A son?

"Harvey, it's time to leave! My luggage is ready!" Stacy called down.

"I've called you a taxi, Stacy. It will be right here!" Harvey had managed to dial the number out of desperation.

"A taxi? Harvey, I cannot wait another moment! I'm already behind schedule!" Stacy appeared frantic. "Please friend, take me to the airport now or I will miss my flight! You promised, Harvey! Why can't Christians ever keep their word?"

Harvey thought, what if she is really making a change in her life. My attitude may draw her back into the life she was giving up to start over. He glanced down the road for any sign on the taxicab and found only a kid riding a bike. "Look Stacy, I'll come up and bring the suitcase down, then help load it in the taxi, then I must say my goodbyes and get home."

As Harvey raced up the stairs and made his way to the open door to look in for the waiting suitcase, Stacy had quickly called the cab company and cancelled the service while she waited behind the door for him.

"Stacy, I don't see it. Where is it sitting?"

"Next to the bed," she whispered behind his neck as she took hold of his privates and instantly recognized his lustful moan she knew would come. Harvey turned to find Stacy, naked and willing.

Present Time

Jeremiah had hoped his father would have more willpower and leave the fallen woman's house. "She tempted him and he gave into her."

"Being a newlywed, your father suddenly had a strong sexual drive and both he and Clara were still students and their finals took most of their time. The drug Stacy used made his need for sex greater. Stacy knew what drugs to use to get her marks hooked and if she noticed it wearing off, she would playfully light up a joint to share then shoot him after he became high. If Harvey would have realized what happened

132

with the laced wine, he could have walked out when it wore off. But that woman is well rehearsed in hooking the man she's after." Jesus just shook his head at Harvey's second chance failure.

"How did Mama find out what happened?" Jeremiah felt both sick and helpless.

"Clara found the apartment empty when she returned that afternoon. She never suspected her dedicated husband whom she had given her heart to, would betray her with another woman. Clara assumed her cousin Daniel had grown worse and Harvey was still by his side. Clara decided to go to the hospital and check on Daniel and see if Harvey was there."

Duke Hospital

Clara made her way quickly to the nurses station and asked how her cousin was doing and if her husband was still there.

"Your poor cousin has taken a turn for the worse, Mrs. Mitchell." The nurse looked up sadly. "But at least Daniel won't have to leave this life on his own, now that you're here."

"Alone? My husband was coming here to sit with Daniel and knowing Harvey, he would never leave with Daniel, his best friend, to take his last breath alone."

"I don't think your caring husband would have left with Daniel's girlfriend if he knew his friend didn't have long to live." The nurse could see Mrs. Mitchell was suddenly upset over the news about her husband's departure from the hospital. "I never meant to upset you dear. It really seemed quite innocent. Daniel's girlfriend came in weeping. We know this because all the monitors placed in the ICU help us watch the patients at all time. Miss Blackwood only came by a couple of times I recall. She never entered his room on her previous visit. She said she was headed back to New York and needed a lift to the airport. Your sweet husband said he would take her if she was ready because he had only one hour before he needed to get home and study."

Clara had learned all the nurses' names on Daniel's floor, so she said softly, "Doris, what time did they leave the hospital?"

The nurse checked their departure time on her chart, then checked her watch and noted it was almost 1:00 PM. "Oh my, time does fly on these shifts. Your husband signed out at 10:00 a.m., three hours ago." The caring nurse reached over to pat her nervous hand. "I just bet if you go home my dear you'll find your husband there waiting and worrying about you."

"Doris, I just came from our apartment and Harvey has not been home. Clara was pale with worry. Did you hear them say that they were headed directly to the airport from here?"

"Come to think of it, this Stacy lady said she had to go back to her flat and get help carrying down her largest suitcase." The nurse felt helpless when she added, "Harvey said they could swing by and get it, then head for the airport." The nurse saw worry written on the beautiful young lady's face. "I am sure everything is fine, my dear. He probably got tied up in heavy traffic."

"That street trash harlot has tricked my husband into going to her apartment!" Clara tried to control her emotions, but she could see what Stacy Blackwood had done to her cousin and now she was hitting on Harvey. "I will find out for myself why Harvey never came home, after I stay with Daniel to let him know how much we love him!"

Daniel's Hospital Room

Clara held her cousin's hand as she sang to him all the songs they used to sing together while growing up in Israel. Daniel slowly opened his eyes to see his precious cousin's tearful face. Daniel felt her love for him and he was grateful he wasn't alone. He managed to smile as he squeezed her hand, drawing her immediate attention, then whispered, "Jesus has made me whole and restored my soul, so I am fit for heaven. The Lord is waiting for me to say my goodbyes, Clara. His angels of light are here to take me home. Tell Harvey not to trust Stacy. They thought I could not hear her act. Tell my friends Harvey and Toby, I will always love them and we shall play that game in heaven. I've always had a special place in my heart for you, sweet Clara, and I love you, little cousin. Daniel closed his eyes in peaceful rest.

The Present Time

"Jesus, did my mama go to Stacy's apartment and find them together?"

"Jeremiah, your beautiful mother did drive to Stacy Blackwood's townhouse and when she saw Harvey's truck parked out front, knowing how many hours he had been there, she knew they were together. Clara sat quietly in her car, her heart breaking as she wept, then she drove away." Jesus knew this would be hard for the young preacher to witness, but he had to know how his father changed.

Cassie felt Jeremy's sadness and took his hand. "Lord we know at some point Clara and Harvey got back together, that things were never the same for them. Most women today would not have given Harvey Mitchell another chance."

"Most women are not like Clara or you, Cassie Mitchell."

Cassie gave Jesus a big smile, knowing she loved Jeremy so much she would forgive him for any mistake he might make.

"They did get back together. After a month of sex and drugs, Harvey ran out of money and Stacy told him she was going back to New York, where men were loaded with cash for drugs and her lifestyle. With a shocked look, Harvey asked her what was he to do. She told him to go home to sweet forgiving Clara, then find yourself a job."

Stacy's Townhouse

"Job? Go back to Clara? That goody Christian Jew?" Harvey tried to hold her back and she pushed him away.

"That's right, Harvey. What choice do you have? To come with me?" Stacy laughed sarcastically. "You are a loser, Harvey, a wasted junkie, a broke slob and just as stupid as your friend Daniel, who actually was one rich Jewish boy until I broke his piggy bank!" She laughed and continued packing her bags.

"You said you loved Daniel, bitch! You said you loved me!" Harvey weaved back and forth.

"Love?" Stacy howled in laughter. "Yeah, loved your money and that hot body until you became a clumsy drunk!"

135

She continued laughing as she shut her last bag. "The only thing I love in this stinking world is myself!" Stacy walked to the window where her cab pulled up. "It appears that long lost cab finally found my house." She let her bag slide down the steps and smiled at her reflection in the wall mirror. "By the way, Harvey, you only have until tonight to be out of my house. I sold it a month ago." She turned to see his crying had turned to anger.

"If you want poor Clara to take you back, you best wash that evil look off your distorted face and wait for the drug to die away, so you can drive that ugly truck out front, if it still starts after sitting there for four long weeks." Stacy opened the door. "Ah, fresh air! A new start with a large bankroll to start with" The wicked woman turned to face him after giving the cab driver a wave to put away her luggage. "A wealthy new mark is awaiting my arrival." She laughed when he tried to stand up. "Poor darling. Don't worry. Dear Clara is probably starving for affection. You can release all that lust on her. Clara is your saintly wife after all, Harvey. Clara will honor her wedding vows."

"Listen, bitch, don't you dare say anything bad about Clara!" Harvey shouted. "She is the lady you will never be!"

"And you will never be the husband poor Clara married, ever again!" She smiled mockingly. "You might find a job working digging ditches. That fits a gutter rat perfect!"

"Get out! I know I was stupid to walk up those stairs after being warned to leave! You are an evil, wicked agent of Satan!" Harvey felt the drug wearing off and considered pushing her down the steps. "I will crawl back into Clara's life if she will have me. I will get a good job to support us! I will clean up my sinful body and return to being the man Clara married!"

Stacy howled loudly and glanced down at the cab driver waiting just outside the open front door. "Look, Harvey, I'm leaving now with lots of money paid to me by the drug dealer I work for. You, on the other hand, have nothing left except that old truck and the drug problem mixed with becoming a full-blown alcoholic. Your sad life will be cut short one day, just like it was for Daniel, who by the way died on the day we left him alone to make out." Once more Stacy prepared to leave, but paused. "By the way, darling, Daniel wasn't alone I hear. Your Clara came, thinking you were still there. She sang to him as he slipped away. I'm sure the nurse told her we left together. I wonder why she never came by to see if you were there."

"I believe Clara did come by the day I left with you, the moment Daniel died. She was clever enough to figure out what was going on behind those closed shutters from the amount of time I had been missing."

"If Clara loved you as much as she claimed, why didn't she come up and confront us?" Stacy thought she had him stumped over his wife's lack of action.

"I'll tell you why my wife left without taking her hurtful revenge on the man's stealer you are! Clara Mitchell is too much a lady to become hostile nor did she want to see the man she thought she could trust having sex with a common whore!"

"You bastard! May your life be miserable with that good woman!" Stacy walked out and slammed the door.

The Dorm Apartment

Clara had tried to keep busy packing their few things around her temporary job. She was about to lose hope over Harvey ever returning home. Even though he had chosen to stay with Stacy, Clara felt a pain of pity for the man she still loved, knowing that, when she had to move out for the cleaning service to make the apartment ready for new students, Harvey would find her missing should he decide to finally come home to her.

Clara sighed as she packed up Harvey's things. She gave a sudden jump when someone knocked on the front door. She checked her watch and knew it was too late for the landlord to be handing out departure notices. Stepping up close to the door, she prayed it was someone she knew instead of the new student family coming by to check out the apartment.

"Yes, who is it?" Clara asked politely hoping it was just a delivery.

"Clara, it's Harvey. May I come in?" He spoke softly.

Clara had longed to hear Harvey's voice once more, and

she closed her eyes at the familiar sound. She had mixed emotions and felt her body trembling as she slowly opened the door, instantly noticing the change in her husband's appearance. He was thinner now, no less from very little food and too much alcohol, drugs and sex.

Harvey also noticed the big change in his wife. She had cut her long hair into a bob, her figure had matured into one of a shapely model, but her most outstanding difference was the bright glow that lit up her angelic face.

"Clara, you look fabulous."

"Harvey, I am overjoyed to see you well, but it appears this woman you chose over me has never fed you right." Clara stood firmly in the doorway. "I guess you have come by for your things."

"My things?" Harvey looked past her to see the stacks of packed boxes. "Clara, are you throwing me out?"

"Harvey, you chose to leave me, remember?" Clara raised her voice. "Your friend's fast girlfriend, the same one that ruined Daniel's young life and killed him!"

Harvey remained silent so his wife could get her anguish out.

"That harlot lured you to her flat, the townhouse that Daniel bought for her when he thought she loved him! Women like that don't know how to love someone! They put on a good show, pretend to be something they're not until they suck you dry of every bit of money you have. Thank God I was smart enough to switch our joint savings to another bank or you would have made me penniless! Don't tell me, let me! After you became worthless to the she-devil, after she had you completely hooked on drugs, alcohol and cheap broads like her sorry ass, Miss Stacy Blackwood walked out on you! Does that sound about right, Harvey Mitchell?"

"I'm afraid so, Clara, but the bitch knew my weakness and she took advantage of my stupidity!" Harvey pushed his way past Clara to open one of the boxes to see what was inside. "Dishes?"

"Harvey, I am packing our things up because I have to move before the month is out." Clara pushed him aside to reclose the box. "This felt like a real home when you were here, but since you're gone and I no longer have your love, it's easier to move."

"Why, Clara? We can make it a home again. Stacy is out of my life for good." Harvey had known things would take time to heal. "Please Clara, give me another chance. I'll get a job! I've changed in some ways, but my love for you will never change. I promise to be a good husband to you again. Please, forgive me! Clara, this is our home, we can make it work out!"

"Harvey, this is a Duke University college dorm apartment. Since we are no longer students here, we must leave so other students can come in." Clara felt some hope for her and Harvey, that they might still have some kind of life together after all. "We cannot stay here any longer. We have to move on."

"Clara, you said 'we' can't stay here and 'we' have to move on." Harvey finally looked hopeful. "Does that mean you will give me another chance, sweetheart?"

"I will, Harvey, for three reasons. One: because I never stopped loving you, even though I cried myself to sleep every night because you were not by my side in bed. Second: Daniel woke up and smiled, then asked me to tell you, please don't let Stacy hurt you like she did me. Then he said he loved you and Toby and would look forward to playing that game with you in heaven. Daniel then gave me my own loving message."

"Daniel awoke? From brain death,? Clara, his brain functions were being monitored on a big screen. There was absolutely no activity shown! I don't understand." Harvey felt guilty for leaving with Stacy and the fact that the fallen woman felt some sort of sick victory that they were making out when she announced, to hurt me, poor Daniel slipped away. "Clara how could Daniel know I left with his ex?"

"First, Daniel awoke because God gave us a healing miracle. Even though my heart was breaking, knowing that you had left with Stacy, I didn't want to leave Daniel alone, to die with no one beside him."

"You are a good woman, Clara." Harvey felt worse, once again knowing what he and Stacy were doing when his best friend was dying.

Joan Byrd

"I took his cool hand and started singing all the songs me and Daniel sang when we were growing up in Israel. Then Daniel opened his eyes and smiled. There was a bright radiance around him as he spoke. Daniel said he could hear everything you and Stacy were saying and he knew she was setting you up just like she did him. He had read through her phony act."

"I feel like I let my buddy down." Harvey dropped his head. I'm a real jerk!

"Yes, you made some bad choices, Harvey. You haven't been on the best behavior for a man who had his heart set on becoming a minister. Clara's eyes lit up with a thought. Harvey, we might not have to move just now if you choose to finish your classes and take the finals. We can still have our dream and be placed at another church."

"That may still be your dream, Clara, but not mine. I'm moving on with something new, more suited to me," Harvey stated bluntly.

"But Harvey you had your heart set on preaching the gospel like Billy Graham, remember?" Clara started to take his hand and he jerked it back. "Listen, Harvey, you did something you're not proud of, but we can get past that when you ask the Lord for forgiveness."

"Clara, I am going to say this only one time, so listen!" Harvey spoke with authority. "I don't want you to mention me becoming anything religious! Understand! I woke up from that so-called dream. My parents weren't wrong after all!"

"Harvey, you cannot be serious! Did that harlot kill your love for the Lord? Did that whore have that much control on you, Harvey Mitchell?"

"Yes, Clara, Stacy made me see the truth. If I wanted a hit or sex, I had to give her what she wanted to hear and it became easier for me to deny my belief for hers, just to get the satisfaction I needed!"

"Was this atheist worth losing your beautiful soul for? Well, I will tell you plainly, Harvey Mitchell, I will never give up my belief in God for you or anyone else! And, if it wasn't for the third reason I chose to stay with you, I might call it quits right now!

Harvey suddenly appeared hurt, as tears filled his eyes. "Clara, please darling, it's the drug speaking. I need you, Clara, I love you! I never stopped loving you, Clara. When my head began to clear, I realized what I had done to you and I felt sick over my weakness." Harvey dropped to his knees, his tears now falling down his pale cheeks. "Clara, I cannot live if you don't want me anymore, don't love me anymore."

"Harvey, I will love you forever and with God's help I will teach our son to love and respect you as well."

"Our son?" Harvey couldn't resist pulling Clara into his arms. "Clara, I promise to be a good husband to you dearest, from now on and be the best daddy ever to our boy."

Back to the Present Time

"But, due to his drinking problem, Harvey wasn't able to hold a job and he fell into the man you remember." Jesus made the past fade away.

"Then, it will be up to me to help you change the outcome of this fatal day that took the life of both my parents." Jeremiah somehow knew the Lord was giving his father another chance to return to him. The young preacher also knew, it was up to him to somehow reverse the past events of what happened so he could help save his father this time from Lucifer's powerful grip. Jeremiah would have put his new skills to the test to defeat the strongest foe on earth, Lucifer, the powerful archangel and God's number one enemy.

CHAPTER 21

Jeremiah found himself ten-years-old again, but this time he was aware what had happened on the previous tenth birthday over twenty-years-ago and he knew the Lord had made it possible for him to actually be able to save his father this time, as well as his precious mama. He waited anxiously as his mama brought over the birthday cake, knowing his angry father would be bursting into the room any second. As his attention stayed on the door he could hear his mama speaking.

"Well darling, do you like your birthday present?" her slim fingers gently turned his face around. "Jeremiah, you must not be nervous about your daddy coming home early. Please relax sweet boy and look at what I got you this year."

"Mama, it is exactly what I wanted but I never expected to get a bat and a ball." Jeremiah swallowed when he heard his father's car drive up, but his mother didn't seem to hear it. "Maybe we had better hide the gifts and cake for a while mama. I heard a car pull in the driveway and it sounded like daddy's."

Before Clara could react to her son's bold statement, the door flung open and Harvey stared over at the happy scene. Words of heated hate flew from his foul mouth and he made his way across the room swaying. He stopped when his young son sang out.

"Daddy, you're just in time! My prayers have been answered!" in total confusion, Harvey watched his boy run over to hug him. "You remembered my birthday daddy! I just knew you would since mama said my gift was from you and her." Real tears came to Jeremiah's eyes as he watched his parents exchange glances. "Mama said it was your idea to have a real birthday party for me with birthday cake and everything." Jeremiah looked over at his mama and gave her a wink, then enjoyed her smile. "Daddy, mama said it was your ideal to give me that bat and ball I've always dreamed of having! You're the best, daddy! Thank you!"

"Jeremiah, I'm pretty sure it was your mama who planned all this for you son." Harvey felt his own tears welling in his eyes as let his fingers brush over the boy's dark hair. "Clara, go ahead and tell the boy the truth."

"Harvey, in a way it was your ideal to get the ball and bat for your son." Clara walked over to joined father and son. "Before things changed Harvey we found out we were having a baby and you were so excited over the possibility of it being a boy, I recall you saying,"

"As soon as our son is old enough, I am going to get him a ball, mitt and bat and teach him how to play baseball." Harvey reached for Clara's hand. "Clara, what happen to me? Where did I go wrong?"

"You thought you were taking a friend to the airport" both Harvey and Clara stopped to stare down at their young son. "You never suspected her as setting a trap for you and you never thought to walk out for fresh air, the first time, until the Lord gave you a second chance. The first life you walked up those stairs when Stacy called you and that is what changed your life and ultimately took both your lives from me."

"Harvey, do not listen to this simple child! You cannot change from the drunk and adulterer you have become!" came the demanding voice. "You turned your back on God, so you no longer belong to him!

You are mine! You can never replace those children's lives you ran over this day!"

"Daddy" Harvey and Clara turned to find their little boy had grown into a handsome man. "The devil would want you to believe his lies but if you clear your head you will recall what really happened to those children standing in the church yard."

"HE KILLED THEM, STUPID MAN! I SET IT ALL IN MOTION SO I COULD TAKE HIS SOUL THIS NIGHT!" Satan screamed.

"No, I never hit anyone or the angels, my old friend Tobi!" Harvey felt Clara take his trembling hand as her husband stared at the evil being. "I remember now! You were seated next to me at the bar, ordering me to have another drink and another.

Then you helped me under the wheel and led me down the wrong road! The church road that was a dead-end, straight for those children and their pastor, my friend."

"It does not wipe out your sins Harvey Mitchell! You turned your back on God, committed adultery against your pitiful wife and left your good friend Daniel to die alone, before I claimed his fried soul!" Lucifer shot fire toward the window and it opened, then turned to stare at Jeremiah. "I had you were I wanted you, twenty-years-ago Jeremiah Mitchell! A frighten little boy who watched helplessly while this man slapped your mama so hard she fell across the room and broke her stupid neck!" Seeing the horror on Clara's face as she suddenly recalled their previous life, Satan curled his snarling lips in a smile. The evil being could see through her flash back as Clara could see herself rushing over to save her little boy from his angry drunk father, trying to stop him by hitting him with the vase he had previously broken when he threw Jeremiah's baseball across the room. Clara recalled the hot fear she had felt when she found herself falling quickly toward the solid wall and quickly whispered for God to save her son, then her world went black, and then came a brilliant light and the face of the Lord.

Lucifer sneered at the last vision from her death and turned back to their son. "Your father had easily killed your poor-weak mama, then he set his thoughts on you, the one thing left standing in his way."

"Don't you mean, the one thing left that was standing in your way, Lucifer?" Jeremiah knew Satan was trying to rattle his resolve as to frighten him, but the young minister was well underway to becoming the Lord's witness for redeeming all those in need by the blood of the lamb. "You knew Harvey Mitchell was one step away from becoming a minister and the he and his loving wife had a church waiting to begin their life together for the Lord's work. You were well aware of Harvey's sex-drive and how he had painfully waited to be with his beloved. The finals were coming up and Clara and Harvey agreed to concentrate on the test so they could graduate, then they would be free to enjoy one another in celebration. You pulled out the great temptation harlot, a gifted actress who could easily fool a man whose best friend was dying and the little whore played the sad lover to the dying friend, which she also happened to get hooked up on drugs, the drugs that you said fried his brain!" Jeremiah could only smile when Lucifer knew he knew all about a man's soul. "That right Lucifer, an overdose of drugs mixed with 100 proof liquor will fry the human brain but the soul cannot be harmed by man or you Satan! It is eternal! Forever! Never to end!"

"So, the soul might live forever, you, Christian puppet, but if that soul belongs to me, and believe me young Mitchell, I have collected many over the many years this earth, which belongs to me, has existed, you can bet those damned souls have been deeply harmed!" Lucifer smiled, as though he had won the debate.

"Your words are weak Lucifer and they hold no true meaning." Jeremiah knew the evil being was stalling for time but the young preacher knew how to alter the outcome in Harvey's favor. "It is true you choose to torture many of your victims while they wait in your hell below while other lost souls wait in a confined underground prison until judgement day. Then all souls will be called up to face the final judgement and that includes you Lucifer and your 10,000 demons! As for Daniel, you claim his brain is fried. The truth is, Daniel was given a miracle. Now his brain has been restored, for he was redeemed by the Blood of the Lamb. He lives in heaven."

Anger showed on the powerful angel's face but he knew this young man was out of his reach, for he could sense the presence of Jesus near-by. "You dare come in and retake that which was mine! A mere man!" His sneer turned to a mocking grin. "You shall fail in this so call mission Jeremiah Mitchell! You are not cut out to save the souls of the lost, the lame, the blind, the cripple, and the mute!"

"No, I cannot save anyone myself, for I am not Holy." Jeremiah remained calm and unafraid. "But, I can and will lead those who are lost, who are lame, those who are blind, those who are cripple or mute and anyone else who needs to be healed or saved, to the healing stream."

"Those you approach with these empty words will kick you from their sight!" Lucifer laughed out.

"Satan, you have lived all these ages and you still do not know the power of the most-high God! Your Creator is still very much in charge of His earth! His universe! His heavenly home!" Jeremiah noticed the devil's evil eyes roll slowly toward Harvey. "Planning your move Lucifer?" like magic, the young minister found himself between Lucifer and Harvey. "You may not take him so quickly as you did before, thinking he was considering stopping his bad reputation and disrespect for his wife and son before it was too late. You grew tense when you heard Harvey asking me to help him as he was spinning dizzy from the hard blow you gave him with my new batt. Then I felt your arms tighten around me, holding me back from running to his aid. There was some type of force that pulled my father toward the open window and now I can remember when he reached out to me asking me to save him, that force jerked his entire body through the window, where I saw him glance down, his eyes filled with horror!"

"And you think that you, Jeremiah Mitchell, a weak human, can keep me, Lucifer, the greatest angel created, from collecting that which belongs to ME?" the fierce voice rang out so loud, Clara and Harvey grabbed their ears. As cold eyes glared down at the young man, Satan raised his hand and sucked Harvey into his grip. "Witness my strength, boy! You cannot defeat me, you fool! HARVEY MITCHELL IS MINE!"

Still calm and filled with peace Jeremiah spoke to his father. "Father, you asked me to help you the first life. Then you asked me to save you. Do you see your mistake with your words sir? Lucifer does not have the power to take you again until you say those final words." Jeremiah looked deeply into his father's eyes. "Remember what you learned in seminary." Jeremiah felt his mother take his hand and he gently squeezed it reassuringly.

Harvey had been shaking in Lucifer's arm but he slowly felt a sudden calm, then a sense of peace. His words came out clear. "Help me son!" tears filled his eyes as he recalled the words he had spoken and he knew now what he should have asked for. "Son, take me to the cross, upon which Jesus died for such a wretch as I, that I might be washed in my Savior's redeeming blood and be healed from my many sins!" Harvey knew he had the right answer this time for he felt Lucifer release him. The grateful man watched as his Clara and his son ran over to hug him.

CHAPTER 22

Marsh Cove, Outer Banks, Messiah Methodist Church

Jeremiah stood staring out at the ocean, Cassie by his side. Ever since his family had been made whole again and he witnessed his life growing up with both parents, his thoughts had turned to Reverend George Russell and his loving wife Nancy. Since his parents had not died, then Reverend Russell could have never found the young runaway and took him in, to both their home and heart. They had adopted him and treated him like the son they had always wanted but were unable to have. The loving adopted parents had paid his way through Duke University, but now that things had changed, what had become of them?

"Jeremy darling, please tell me what is bothering you." Cassie gently touched his serious face. "Maybe I can help with this problem?"

"Cassie, I never considered that if you make one change in pass mistakes you could be altering other people's lives." Jeremiah looked down, sadness filling his eyes. "The lives of two very precious people in my life."

"Oh darling, you are referring to George and Nancy Russell, aren't you?" Cassie felt his pain.

"They had adopted me and treated me like their very own son, showing me more love than many real parents show their own children." Tears collected in his eyes. "I wanted for nothing and they made me feel special. I had just loss my parents, both in horrific deaths and ran away from the orphanage the moment they took me in. George found me camped out under the big boxwood by the church doors where I had been living ever since I ran away from that home for orphans." Jeremiah's eyes dropped on his hands. "They paid my way through college then Duke divinity school or at least they did until everything was reversed and gaining back both my parents what did I leave them with? Those same two people longing for a child but never received that blessing after all?"

"Jeremiah, standing here worrying about all the what if's is not the solution darling." Cassie took his hand again. "The only way you will ever know how things turned out for them is to go and see them. I could see how much they loved you Jeremy when we had to leave for the Holy Lands. Sweetheart, do you believe the Lord is going to just restore your family and leave the Russell's heartbroken?"

Jeremiah paused, and glanced down at the woman he had fallen in love with, and smiled. "My Cassie, is so wise and smart. You're right, we serve a loving and caring God. He wouldn't leave them without a child to call their own."

"Well, finally you know what to do, to learn what happened to alter their lives." Fran appeared, once again, dressed like the shell lady, causing the couple to jump. "I never meant to startle you lovebirds, but time is ticking and the Russell's home is just across from the Methodist church as you recall."

"I take it the Lord is ready for us to return to Nazareth, dear friend." Jeremiah gave the loving angel a hug. "And you are right as usual. The only way to know the answer is to go to the source and find out first hand."

"Children, take my hands and we can go there quickly." With faith-filled trust, Jeremiah and Cassie did not hesitate to take her hand and they found themselves on the Russell's front porch, directly in front of the front door. Fran glanced down at the doorbell, blinked, and smiled when it rang out, then vanished.

The door opened and George laughed out before grabbing the young man. "Jeremiah, Tommy, the young teen that mows our lawn told me and Nancy he thought he saw you down on the beach with your pretty lady!" the Methodist minister stood back and waved them inside, before calling for his wife. "Nancy, set that pan off the burner and come in here."

Nancy came through the kitchen door and after seeing who had rang the bell, she raced over to give them both a hug. "You're back dear! I never dreamed you would return this quick. Is your mission over already? Your last letter stated after being healed by the blood of the Lamb, the Lord led you to some kinsmen in Nazareth to start your new mission."

"Nancy, I just concluded my very first mission project, right here in Marsh Cove." Jeremiah had been trying to read their action toward him and he had felt the same incredible love from them as it was before, when he left. "Cassie and I will be heading back to Israel within the hour." His next statement would spark their place in his new life. "We just left my parents home with our farewells, but I could never leave the Island without coming by to see two of my favorite people. What you both did for me throughout my youth and maturing years has touched me deeply." His emotions were honest and completely loving. "You have always been my second-set of parents who treated me like I was your own son and I could not love you more if I tried, Daddy George, Mama Nancy."

Cassie was fighting her own tears as she witnessed the deep devotion and love the couple felt for her Jeremiah, when they wrapped their arms around him crying.

"Jeremiah, when your daddy changed back to the man he was when your beautiful mama married him, they asked me and Nancy to be your godparents and we felt the Lord had finally blessed us with a child to help parent." George related the unknowns to the young man. "When Harvey chose to return to Duke to get his divinity degree, he needed to take a refresher course and he needed his wife by his side. They asked us to watch you for those six months since you were in school here at the cove, and Nancy and I jumped on it. We did everything together on the weekends, Saturdays and after church services, do you remember?"

"Yes, I remember those outings well, daddy!" Jeremiah enjoyed George's big smile. "Picnics, with mama's great cooking!" he winked at Nancy. "You teaching me how to fish and swim, at the town pool. Going to movies and the Marsh Cove Fair." Jeremiah took Cassie's hand. "When we have our own son, I can teach them everything you taught me and tell them that their Grandpa and Grandma Russell taught me everything that makes life happy."

Back on the Beach

"Now, you know Jeremiah Mitchell, just how happy you made George and Nancy Russell as well as your own parents." Fran had brought them back to the beach after their tearful goodbyes. "The fact that you were such a loving young man made it easy to make everyone feel loved as parents."

"As long as everyone turned out happy, Fran, then I am satisfied and ready to return to our mission." Jeremiah looked out at the vast Atlantic Ocean and watched a flock of Seagulls fly into formation to form a cross. His eyes glistened with fresh tears. "Cassie, it is time. The mission to guide those seeking redemption is at hand. We must follow the cross to find the Lord's redeeming blood left behind."

"Right after I perform one small ritual for you both, right here on this moonlit beach." Jesus had appeared with a lovely trio of angelic musicians seated in front of three solid gold harps. "It is time to combine your hearts as one."

Jeremy and Cassie had been totally surprised by the happy announcement, overjoyed to become husband and wife at last. To have their Lord perform their ceremony made the wedding far greater than anything they could have hoped for. An array of flowers from heaven had appeared round and about them as the harps played glorious music composed by the Master's hand. With his beautiful words to bind them as one, Jesus' little touch formed them together as one and pronounced them husband and wife. The loving Lord lifted their hands to kiss.

"Now you are wed and from this day are Jeremy and Cassondra Mitchell. All your things have been sent to your new home in Nazareth. You must wait a little while longer to seal your marriage vows, for your kinsmen are expecting your return. No one needs ever to dispute your vows being legal in this world, for I am the Lord your God, the Maker of all perfect laws. Should any man approach you wrongly, show him your wedding bands, sealed in heaven."

Jesus gave them a perfect smile and released their hands so they could see the rings. He had miraculously placed heaven's rings on them. Jeremy had a solid gold band with a crystal cross embedded on the top. Cassie had gasped in amazement for finding the Blue Royal ring shining on her left finger.

After revealing their incredible rings to one another, the happy couple heard Jesus say as he vanished with the flowers, harps and angelic musicians, "You may kiss your bride, Jeremy, and Fran, you may wipe your tears away and prepare for travel."

"It was a beautiful heavenly wedding, dear ones." Fran stepped between them, gave them a bright smile before taking the couple's hands. "It is time to return to Nazareth, you love birds."

The married couple vanished with one jolly angel.

CHAPTER 23

Nazareth

After finally making love for the first time, the Mitchell's had settled in the House of Jesu and were up the following morning, rested and renewed. Memmi and Simon had been up before the sun rose and where waiting in the small kitchen for the young couple, breakfast made and laid out on the small harvest table.

"I can see you both had a restful night so with your bellies full with my Memmi's warm breakfast you may begin your search of the remanence of our Savior's holy blood." Simon spoke his words as though he had just invited them to go shopping with them or perhaps take the day to go fishing, not something as powerful as looking for the blood of Jesus left here over 2,000-years-ago. "The older gentleman pulled out a chair for his wife, then Cassie before nodding to the far end chair meant for Jeremiah. "We are aware that you have witness Jesus's past come to life in many places while the Holy Week drifted by. Finding the many places where the saving blood rest is the fun part of this amazing job. Once you know where all the remanences are, then the Lord will guide those seeking healing to you and whatever their particular need is, then the Spirit will reveal which place to take them for healing." Simon spoon what looked like oatmeal in his mouth and between bites asked, "Do you have any questions for me before you two get started on the remanence search?"

"What exactly are we looking for Uncle Simon and where, Jerusalem, where our Lord was crucified?" Jeremiah stirred the oatmeal-looking mash in his bowl. "Memmi, you wouldn't happen to have some cinnamon and cream for this oatmeal, would you?"

The couple couldn't resist their laughter before the older woman past him some fresh home-churn butter. "Forgive our laughter young Jeremiah, but you mistake my potato mush for this American oatmeal. This good butter will go far better in my good mush along with a big slice of my warm bread and fig jelly."

"Yes, this is very good Memmi and very feeling like Uncle Simon stated." The handsome minister gave his host a wink then turned to his uncle. "Are these remanences in old Jerusalem, where Jesus was flogged, crowned with sharp thorns and then nailed painfully on that Roman cross?"

"Yes, some of those objects, mostly garments and clothes, can be located in the area, although the Holy Blood left on the steps of Pontius Pilate palace are no longer in Jerusalem. The Roman Catholic Church had them moved to the Vatican. The many visitors to visit the little church inside the large Vatican, crawl up the steps out of respect for our Savior's great sacrifice and drops of dried blood can be seen moving up the steps."

"Now that you mention it, I do recall watching a program revealing several items the church claim to have been connected to Jesus." Cassie joined in the conversation. "There is a part of the manger where the baby Jesus was laid, a Roman nail, thought to have been one of the nails driven in our loving Lord. An old piece of wood, thought to be part of the cross where Jesus hung and a thorn from the sharp crown that he wore." Cassie gently tapped her spoon as she thought. "And remanence of the sign Pilate had ordered to be placed above the Savior's head."

"Then the Roman Church has some bloodstain items, but things like the manger and the sign could be ruled out for places with the blood of the lamb." Jeremiah added. "all worthwhile and important but irrelevant to our mission." He fastened his eyes on his uncle. "You said some of the items, mostly garments and clothes could be found in old Jerusalem, so you are telling me Jesus left remanences of his everlasting blood in several locations throughout the Holy Lands?"

"Smart boy and if you can recall the many places where you saw our beloved Savior come to life again, from the past of course, then I might suggest starting there." The wise man's eyes twinkled as he asked. "Dear boy, I dare say you were given a sign in the heavens before you departed your homeland, did you not?"

"Now, how on earth could you have known that Uncle Simon, unless that sweet shell angel arrived here first." Jeremiah couldn't miss the couple's exchanging smiles. "Is seeing the sign of the cross created by a flock of white Seagulls something you both experienced before you began your mission?"

"Almost the same Jeremiah, only our cross came in the form of white doves." Memmi smiled. "Then white roses, Love birds, white clouds and all kinds of beautiful white things, all forming a holy cross."

"Oh, I get it!" Cassie laughed. "When Jeremy and I arrive at the correct spot, some type of white cross will appear in front of us!"

"My dear boy, you have got a very intelligent young wife there!" Uncle Simon stood up and walked to the door, then opcncd it to a clear-sunny day. "Lovely day for a remanence discovery and since you are already in Nazareth, extremely close to your first find, I would say here is as good a place to start as any."

"The boyhood home of Jesus!" Jeremiah took his wife's hand and thanked his extended family for the meal and guidance, then started down the path until they reached the familiar grounds. "This looks familiar." His attention fell down the path to the shady opening. "I believe Joseph's Carpenter Shop was in that clearing but there's no sign of a cross." He felt Cassie touch his shoulder, and he turned to see what had drawn her attention. The fluttering of white butterflies swirled up until they formed a perfect cross and stood over what appeared to be a grownup path.

The couple made their way quickly to the path and instantly heard the sound of childhood laughter. Glancing briefly at each other, they made their way down the now cleared path toward the voices until they spotted a young boy with long brown hair and a smaller girl who was pointing down the path.

"Look Jesus, the path is straight here. Let us have a race to see who can reach the apple tree first."

"It might not be safe for us to run Joanna." The sweet calm voice of Jesus spoke as he gave the girl a soft pat of her head.

"I can see stones along the path. You might take a bad fall and hurt yourself."

"I run here with my brother and I simply jump over the stones when one gets in my way. I am a good-fast runner Jesus." Joanna giggled. "Have you ever run before?"

"Of course, I have run these paths and hills many times Joanna, but I am older than you and it would not be a fair race."

"Then, you can do like my brother does. He is your age and he always gave me a head start." Her big blue eyes gaze up. "Please Jesus. I promise to be careful."

"Well, it is against my better judgement young lady, but alright." Jesus looked up the path and saw the stones were spread out evenly, so taking a deep breath he announced, "I shall give you a minute's head start and count slow. Ready?"

"All ready!" She smiled happily and faced the trail.

"Then it is, ready-set-go!" Jesus watched his young friend take off as he slowly counted to sixty then started running down the path watching the young Joanna running and jumping over the stones. Keeping his eyes trained on his friend and dashing around the loose rocks, Jesus suddenly sensed some type of danger ahead and yelled for the little girl to slow down her pace.

"So, you can catch me Jesus!" Joanna called back laughing, knowing he had given her twice the time to get ahead as her brother's twenty-five seconds count. "A few more yards and I shall be at that apple tree having a big juicy apple!"

Seeing the large stone in front of her as she looked back laughing, Jesus called out a warning. "Joanna, the stone! Look out!" She turned in time to see the stone but lost her balance and started tumbling off the path into the underbrush. Suddenly, a loud scream could be heard as Jesus raced toward his little frighten friend.

"Hold on Joanna! Do not move, I am coming!" staring straight ahead, the scared young Jesus forgot the large stone was in His path and suddenly as he felt his foot strike it, the Son of God heard scripture running through his head, "FOR IT IS WRITTEN, HE SHALL PUT HIS ANGELS CHARGE OVER THEE, TO KEEP THEE: AND IN THEIR HANDS

THEY SHALL BEAR THEE UP, LEST AT ANY TIME THOU
DASH THY FOOT AGAINST A STONE!" and as thought he
moved in slow motion, Jesus could feel strong hands lifting
him over the stone and back safely on the path, where the
young girl stumbled off.

Taking a deep breath, Jesus raced into the bramble and
found Joanna, dangled up in a large briar vine that had wrapped
around her beautiful face. The young girl cried out in pain.

"Please hurry Jesus! Take this sharp thorny vine off my
face!" she was bleeding badly and Jesus knew her face had
been torn all over. "Jesus, are you there? I cannot see you! Did
the thorns poke my eyes?"

"Joanna, I am here and everything will be alright pretty
girl." Jesus quickly reached for the thorns and despite his own
pain from the thorns, his first concern was for the scared child.
"You cannot see me because the blood from the thorns over
your face has ran into your eyes. Just keep them closed until I
remove the thorns and get you free."

"Jesus, will I be scared for life?" Joanna cried as though her
heart was breaking. "When I grow up, you will think I am too
ugly to be your friend."

"Joanna, you will always be my pretty little friend and after
I get you all cleaned up, I promise you will look like new!"
Jesus reassured her and helped her up to clean the blood away
from her eyes. Joanna blinked a few times before the handsome
young boy came into view and her attention fell on his bloody
hands.

"Oh! Sweet Jehovah! You are hurt Jesus! Because of me!"
the young caring girl quickly removed her head covering and
commenced to wiping the blood from Jesus's sacred hands as
He watched her with loving eyes and he gently took the cloth
from her fingers and started cleaning off her bloody face and
the miracle of His life-saving blood completely healed her
beautiful face, as though nothing happened.

Joanna did not need to feel of her face to know some
blessing had just happened, because her eyes were drawn on
the perfect hands of Jesus, bearing no scars or scratches.

The past faded from the quiet couple's view and they found

themselves standing in the overgrown path. Cassie broke their silence.

"Young Joanna could not part with the head covering that held the blood of her best friend Jesus. She had witness the miracle she was a big part of."

"So, when we find the blue head covering for a small girl nearby, it will be our first mission place." Jeremiah saw a vison of a dwelling appear down from the carpenter's dwelling and knew where the young Joanna lived. He pointed toward the empty spot. "The child lived there so that is where we shall find her head wrap, covered with the master's blood."

A middle-aged woman appeared from the wooded area. "Excuse me, but aren't you Jeremiah Mitchell, whose mother is from the house of Jesu?"

He exchanged glances with Cassie before answering the woman dressed in a long gown and wore a headwrap, much like the young Joanna. "I am Jeremiah Mitchell, here on a mission for the Lord, Jesus Christ."

"Then you have just been blessed with the past vision of my long-ago ancestor, Joanna and a ten-year-old Jesus, when He healed her thorn torn face and prevented it from scaring up her incredible pretty face." She gave them a warm smile. "Joanna was only five when Jesus was watching her and the sweet young girl had always known that she loved Jesus and had dreamed of becoming his bride when she reached fourteen. This is why she placed that headwrap in a safe place for a treasured keepsake and after learning who her friend really was, she passed it down for generations to witness the life-saving blood of God's Son, our crucified Savior."

"Then, you have Joanna's headwrap now?" Cassie admired the one atop the woman's head. "Young Joanna's looked very much like the one you wear, only hers was blue."

"My wrap is very similar to my ancestor Joanna's, but not as priceless as the one she possessed." She waved her hand down the path she had come from. "My name is Sharon. Our home lies just down that pathway, so whenever you need the sacred headwrap for a healing, just come by. Heaven's angels will alert us of your need and arrival time, so there is no need to check-in ahead. Young servant of the Most High-God, all who possess articles of Christ Healing Blood, will also be a part of your mission." Sharon gave a loving smile. "Go now! The shop of Joseph will be your next stop before you return to the home of Simon Jesu. God bless you Jeremiah and Cassondra Mitchell on this Holy Mission Journey and may He keep you in His safe keeping." Without another word, the stranger with long-blonde hair disappeared down the path.

CHAPTER 24

Near the Shop of Joseph

"Cassie, I recall seeing the vision of Joseph and Jesus near this spot, where the clearing is." Jeremiah scanned the area with his eyes as his ears listened closely for the familiar sound of carpenter's tools being used. "Sweetheart, do you hear anything resembling hammers or sawing?"

Cassie tilted her head as a faint humming sound filled her senses. "Do you hear what sounds like a constant hum?" she glanced up at her new husband to find him staring in the direction of the noise. "Could that have been something a carpenter might use 2,000-years-ago?"

"It is a grinding wheel Cassie, most likely used for sharping tools." Jeremiah's eyes lit up when the past came to life before him. "It is a grinding wheel! I can see Joseph seated on a stool, his feet on a paddle, paddling the big wheel as he sharpened his ax, most likely used for several purposes." He took his bride's hand. "Can you see him?"

Cassie smiled and squeezed Jeremiah's hand when the ancient scene came into view. "Praise God, yes darling, I see him clearly, as though I could just reach out and touch him and the young man seated with his back to us. One of his other sons, you think?"

"Well, it's not Jesus, so it must be." Jeremiah breathed in the fresh shavings on the floor. "I cannot get over how everything comes back to life, even the smells and sounds." The wheel stop spinning when Joseph stop paddling and rubbed his finger carefully along the sharp edge, then gave his companion a grateful smile.

"Son, I can now shave the bark off the next log and commence to building a third bench." Joseph gently laid the sharp ax down on his work table and walked over to pick out a good-straight log then carried it over and started shaving the bark off. "How is the sanding coming there Simon?"

Jeremiah's ears perked up, knowing this son was his actual ancestor.

"I do not believe that I can get this board any smoother if I were at it all day, father." Simon ran his hand across the wood, then picked up the cleaning cloth and wiped off the sawdust, then laid the finished board aside and picked up one of the bench's legs, still in the rough stage. "Is the smaller hatchet been sharpened lately father? This small work needs nothing larger, does it?"

"Your brother sharpened it last evening before he quit for the night so it must be treated with respect Simon." Joseph glanced up when he heard Simon laugh. "I am quite serious son. Sharp tools are to be respective so take short swings, like I have been doing with this ax."

"Then it will be short swings father." Simon hopped up to retrieve the small hatchet and turned the handle around in his tan hand. "So small and innocent looking, like my Roseland."

"And like your Roseland, too sharp to touch and painfully dangerous if you make the wrong move with her." Jesus had walked up behind his brother and overheard the conversation with their father. The special elder son tapped his brother's head playfully. "And for your own good brother, take you mine off of that woman while you are using a sharp tool!"

"I suppose that is why you have never hurt yourself out here, brother Jesus." Simon picked back. "I have never heard you, not one time, mention any of the available ladies in Nazareth as striking your fancy.

Not even the very beautiful Joanna, who, by the way, is pining for one Jesus."

Jesus caught his father's eyes, who had known the truth about Jesus and who and what He really was. Joseph turned to his outspoken son.

"Simon, just work on your own bad relationship son, which appears is not going anywhere." The ever-watchful father glanced at his son's swing with the hatchet growing higher. "And, your brother is right! Keep your mind on what you are doing." Joseph relaxed when the hatchet was lowered.

"Sure, I am aware I am chasing after a speeding flame."

Simon blew out his breath. "It would appear all the available young women in Nazareth have their eyes set on the one man that is not interested in women." He gave a muffled laugh. "Even my flickering flame, Roseland. When I am with her all she can talk about is Jesus. How tall he is! How handsome he is! What a perfect husband he would make! How perfect he is! What beautiful children he would provide!"

"Brother Simon, I happen to know Claudia, the tool makers daughter, has her eyes set on you." Jesus needed for the subject to end, so he would direct him to his future wife. "Whenever I meet her on the streets, she always asked about you Simon."

"Claudia? That little kid with long-black hair?" Simon glanced over and laughed. "Now, how long would I have to wait to ask that child to marry me?"

"You may ask the very beautiful fifteen-year-old Claudia to court you brother, before some other fellow steals her heart away from you because you are still chasing some girl you will never catch." Jesus walked over to get his heavy apron and strapped it on.

"Fifteen? Beautiful?" Simon stopped shaving the wood and glanced up at his brother's loving smile. "She really does ask about me, Jesus?"

"Simon, has your brother ever lied to you about anything?" Joseph had been listened to his sons and added. "If I were you, young man, I would wake up from that dream over someone you can never have and go get that lovely young lady who loves you."

Simon gave a big smile. "Then, with your permission father, I shall go and call on Claudia this night and asked her to come and dine with us this Saturday, if that suits mother."

"Your mother would be happy to see you finally settling down with a sweet Jewish young woman from a respectable family." Joseph finally asked Jesus the question he had been waiting for. "I see the three pieces I sent you off to rid us of was not with you when you returned. Jesus, it only took you one time-out to find someone who would have it." Joseph gave him a slight shrug before shaking his head. "I have tried to sale those imperfect pieces ever since I made them when I was an apprentice just learning the craft from my own father." The experienced carpenter gave a chuckle when he recalled his parent's action when observing them. "After mother stopped laughing, she told father to have them broken down before someone saw their son's bad attempts at building. Father, through his great smile, informed mother that when their son Joseph became the best carpenter in all Nazareth, they would be worth something, but until then, we shall keep them hidden away out of sight." Joseph reached over to pat his special's son's back. "So, not hearing the sound of jingling in your pocket Jesus I take it you received just the one coin."

Simon chuckled, recalling the misfit threesome. "I would bet brother Jesus could only squeeze a mite from the customer that saw them as dried kindling to start their winter stove."

"You are both wrong about my charming customers." Jesus produced a brilliant smile. "Both ladies were very happy to receive the master carpenter's first pieces. Neither grateful woman saw any of the defects you saw father. They could only see the beauty of each piece that was always hidden from the eye of a perfectionist who made them."

"Then, tell me the names of such charming ladies that now own my first three disasters." Joseph took a seat on his work stool, his eyes still focused on the tall-handsome young man with the most amazing eyes of any man. "It is obvious they both live here in Nazareth, so I must know of them."

"You know of both beautiful ladies father and one of them quite well." There was a twinkle in the blue-green eyes. "You have been sharing a bed with her for almost thirty-years."

"Mary?" Joseph rose up from the stool, his attention went toward their home. "Thirty-years have already past since my beloved conceived you Jesus?" tears of reality in gulf Joseph's dark brown eyes as he reached for his special son's hand. "Which one of those ridiculous pieces did she take?"

"Mother said you had told her everything about your first tries at woodworking and how your parents reacted and when she asked you to show her the pieces, she said you would not allow her to see them. She asked to go with me because she insisted she knew the perfect person to have table and the stool.

The small chest touched mother's heart, because she could see, as she so elegantly put it, 'I can see my Joseph in this precious chest. The carving of a little white lamb in a field of green grass.'" Jesus could tell Joseph had been deeply touched by his wife's deep devotion for him. "Mother pointed out the small house on the edge of town, kissed me, pointed out the one short leg on the table, then the three short legs along side of one long leg on the stool, and after reading her eyes, she waved and walked back to the market while I took care of the misfits then went to the widow Tanner's small dwelling."

"Ester, the Tanner's widow?" Joseph knew the dear woman lived mostly on handouts since her husband squandered all his money away down at the town tavern before passing away, leaving her without their home, furnishings or money. The town council saw fit to help the widow by giving her the run-down, abandon shack on the edge of town. "I suppose that poor soul could pay nothing more than a mite."

"Father Joseph, I took no money from the widow. I told her it was a gift from the house of Joseph, the carpenter." Jesus pulled out his pockets to show they were empty. "Sir, you are the best salesman I know and you failed at ever try. You asked me to get rid of them for you and I merely gave them to someone who now cherishes both the fine table as well as its matching stool."

"You are saying, Ester actually liked those pieces, even with their flaws?" Joseph tried to wrapped his mind around why he had not just offered the pieces to a needy person himself. Perhaps, he thought, it was the voice of his father that made him sell everything he made as he could hear his echo.

"Now Joseph, there may come a time a poor soul approaches the shop and asked for a handout. We must overlook the sadness on their face and refuse, but we must always get some type of payment from every customer, either money or needed items."

"Father, did you hear what I said? You seem to be far away." Jesus had reached over to get his earthly father's attention, and Joseph looked up smiling.

"I think you said something like, the widow placed a vase

of flowers on the table." He suddenly could vision what must have happened when the vase started sliding off the one-sided table. "Son, did you try and stop the widow before she broke her vase?"

"I had no reason to stop her father for the table looked quite lovely after she placed her precious mother's cloth on it then the cherished vase and wild flowers we found behind her small hut." Once again, a twinkle formed in the loving eyes of Jesus.

"Brother Jesus, are you telling me and father a table with three long legs and one short leg stood straight enough to hold an old lady's vase of flowers?" Simon could not control his laughter. "And, every time she sits down to eat on that stool with three short legs and one long one, the poor beggar will end up eating off the floor!"

"Tell me brother, is your heart always cold and without compassion for the less fortunate or is your fable attempt at being cute?" Jesus knew his brother was in need of a lesson from heaven. "The lady I gave these gifts too was both appreciative and joyful, praising God for His goodness and showing blessings to those whose generosity for freely giving to the less fortunate, will benefit greatly in the Almighty's glorious kingdom." Jesus smiled, recalling his mother's innocent suggestion to fix the problem. "I will say this one time and there will be no discussions after as to how or when, just except my words as truth, for you are aware I have never told a lie, for it is not in me to bear false witness." Jesus could read their anxious waiting for his remark so He continued. "When I left the shop with the table and the stool, they were exactly as you described them Simon. But, when I arrived at the widow's home, the table had four short legs as did the matching stool, which worked out perfectly for the short widow." Jesus could see questions forming on his brother's face but the Son of God's earthly father instantly knew that somehow this special son had performed a miracle for this poor lady, who needed the items he had made.

"You did right by those misfits Jesus and I am happy for the widow Mason." Joseph returned to his ax and picked it up. "Sometimes receiving a grateful thank you is payment enough."

"That is right father Joseph as well as the grateful hug the dear lady gave me before I departed her door." Jesus heard his brother gasp out and turned to see him making a face.

"Good heavens Jesus, you actually let that dirty old woman give you a hug?" Simon shook his head. "I just realized who this widow Mason is. That old bat that stands on the street corner in those dirty-dingy rags begging for scraps of food or what ever the unfortunate passerby can afford to give her!" Simon held his nose. "Did she leave her stench on you brother? Yuk!"

"Simon, have you finished down grading a child of God?" Jesus noticed the uncertain expression on Simon's face. "That dear person may wear old-ragged clothes Simon, that have faded with years of washing. I would dare say that Ester Mason smells far better than you do at this very moment brother. Making her own soap from roses, water and flax-wax, the dear lady smelled of mother's favorite flower. The trouble with you brother Simon is you look on the person's outside! How they look, how they dress, what they have or do not have. You must do as the Father in heaven does brother and look on the inside. That part that shows love instead of hate. A person's heart and soul are what makes them beautiful, not that which can be seen from the outside." Jesus moved over to his brother, who had lowered his head in shame, and the loving hand of Jesus lifted his brother's head. "Simon, lessons to the ones we love, come only from the heart. You are my earthly brother and my love for you is boundless. I only desire that you and my brethren live as the Father in heaven leads us to live. I merely show you the way."

"And I am forever grateful for your faithful guidance my brother." Simon gave Jesus a hug. "I shall treat the widow Mason as a child of God, from this day forward and when her soft-rose-silk hand is out on the corner, I shall give her whatever I can. That is a promise."

"Now that everyone understands about loving everyone, it is time to finish our day's work before your mother has our supper ready." Joseph reached up to hang the sharpened ax in its leather sleeve. "There, safe and sound."

"It does not appear to be safe and sound father Joseph."

Jesus grew concern with the sharp ax hanging just above the wall where each male member of the family walked under throughout the day. "With the looks of the old strap I would say it has had better days."

"Jesus, perhaps you could say that about me but not that fine piece of leather up there." Joseph laughed off the possibility of the sharp object falling. "I have been working here since I was a lad son and my father's old leather strap lasted a good-many-years before I toss it in the worn-out tin and fasten a wider one up there in it's place. You night remember the day since you had been observing my actions all day when my dearest Mary brought you out to start learning the trade."

"I was four father Joseph and I can still see you on that stool fastening the strap up before swinging on it to make sure it would hold the lighter tool." Jesus noticed his brother get up to retrieve the two-edge hatchet before returning to his stool. "Simon, what was wrong with the single hatchet? It will prove just as sufficient at shaving the bark off that spinal and not half as dangerous."

"Father, will you inform my over protective brother that I have mastered the use of this very helpful tool." Simon tossed the handle from hand to hand, then sized up the first carved stool leg before glancing up at his special brother. "Now, you are aware this order of stools is being made for the town tavern and Clarence expects only the finest work from the house of Joseph. So, I have to get this wood smooth and with absolutely no splinters or some drunk will come after us if he sticks one up his sorry rear."

Jesus and Joseph glanced at each other trying hard not to laugh. "Just be extra careful with that two-sided weapon and do not let your mind wonder on this new lady friend you plan to call on." Joseph studied for a second what tool he wanted then walked under the hanging rack to the smaller tool storage. Before he could withdraw the smaller scrapper, there was a ripping sound causing the seasoned carpenter to look up only to see the ax hurling down toward his face.

CHAPTER 25

"Father!" Jesus called out loudly as a startled Simon looked up in shock, then watched his older brother move with lightening speed to reach out and catch the sharp blade down in his hands. Joseph watched anxiously as blood ran down the strong-tan-arm of Jesus. Ripping off his sash, the anxious father twirled the long cloth securely around the beautiful wounded hands of his elder son.

"Jesus, please sat down son while I go for the town physician!" the helpless father felt his heart racing knowing how close he came to having his head cut-off. He looked over to find his other son in a wide-eyed shock. "Snap out of it Simon and help your brother until I come back!"

"Come back?" Simon, now startled alert to the reality of what nearly happened and what had actually happened to his perfect brother. Without thinking about the dangerous hatchet, he clutched tightly, Simon jumped quickly from his stool causing it to flip over sending the double blade hatcher straight for his right ear. The severe pain of almost slicing off his ear brought out a loud cry as he sank to the floor holding his wounded ear.

"Simon, hold tight on your ear and do not let go until I say so." Jesus glanced down at his worried father and helped him have a seat, then raced over to his brother, removing the sash from his own wounds. Jesus quickly folded the cloth into a thick square, exposing His-life-saving-blood next to Simon's hand. "Simon, can you hear me speak in your right ear?"

Simon tilted his left ear toward Jesus, his face drawn in a painful expression. "Jesus, did you ask me something in my right ear?" he cried out. "I cannot hear anything brother!"

Jesus raised his voice as to be heard from his left ear. "Simon, remove you hand so I may heal your ear." Jesus noticed his brother's hesitation to take his hand of his ear, perhaps thinking if he held it there it would not fall off. "Simon, do you trust me? Do you trust my word brother?" Jesus was relieved to see Simon moved his head slowly in a positive. "Then, move your hand away and I promise your ear will be better than new. Trust me and I will heal you."

This time Simon removed his hand and Jesus quickly laid his blood-stain cloth over the wounded ear and when he removed the cloth, the ear had been completely healed.

Joseph had been watching in solemn wander as the Son of God performed His miracle right before the carpenter's frightful eyes. As Joseph stared at Simon's perfect right ear and heard his gleeful cry of gratefulness, his attention quickly turned on the perfect hands of Jesus as he watched Him fold the blood-stain cloth. There was no sign of the deep cuts that seemed to cut right through his perfect's son's sacred hands. Slowly rising from his stool on shaky legs, Joseph fell into deep thoughts.

"Will my first son   will God's only Son have a book of scriptures written about Him? Surely the long-awaited Messiah will receive a new book, a testament about His life on earth. Messiah, God with us! How many miracles has He already performed with no one to document them? Jesus had been different from the rest of the human race from the start. Who will tell His story? How will they know about all the important things that we saw over the years from being with this special boy? Surely the Almighty God who spoke to Moses and all the prophets, giving them the words to write down for the Holy Scriptures read with reverence every sabbath in the temple, will fill the ear of a true believer."

Jesus had been taking in his earthly father's thoughts about him and slowly made His way over to place the soiled sash in his hands. "Father Joseph, what you witness today was a blessing from my heavenly Father, so when you shower your grateful praises, give them to Him. I prayed and He answered." Jesus took his trembling hand. "I will not always be here for my family, therefore, if any member of this household, find them self in overpowering troubles that appear to big to move, then lift up your voice in sincere prayer, straight from your heart and soul and with such faith dwelling within you, that problem which you faced as impossible, will lift away by the grace of God. For nothing is impossible for God." Jesus looked deep inside those of his loving earthly father as He spoke softly.

"My life here with you and Mary, my family and friends, my neighbors and kinsmen, have fled passed quickly but our times together will live within my heart for all eternity. Soon I leave to start my mission on earth and the reason for my coming. There are twelve men, chosen by us, the Holy Trinity, at the moment living their own lives and going about their daily business. Before this year is out, I will call them to follow me and with not any reluctance they will leave everything they knew and follow as my disciples. It will be some of them that will write my life's story on earth and call them The Gospels and many generations later all who read what will be called: The Holy Bible, will learn of me from cradle to cross, from birth to death, then to resurrection of life eternal!" Jesus could see the last statement made a profound impact on his earthly father. "Dear love one, I am the good shepherd and the good shepherd lays His life down for His sheep."

"This is why the Messiah, the Son of God, is known as the lamb of God?" Joseph had tears falling as he sadly realized the lamb of God, perfect and without blemish, was the sacrificial lamb for all mankind. "My beautiful son, is there no other way. All who know you are aware there are no sins in you."

"Can the Son of God sin against His Father?" Joseph noticed a heavenly light radiate over the head of Jesus. "Can the Almighty God sin against Himself?"

Once again, reality began to sink inside the very soul of Joseph as he whispered. "Forgive me Jesus, for you have been beside me these thirty-years, I believed you to be my own flesh and blood. I know my heart should not show favors with my children or my beloved Mary, but I, I have always loved you more than anyone! Jesus, is this wrong to feel more love for you than even the young woman I fell so deeply in love with?"

Jesus wrapped his arms around His earthly father as His own tears mingled with Joseph's. "Joseph, I have never witnessed more love for his family and wife like you bestow on your own. Your heart has always been in the right place beloved. It is a right and just thing to place your God first in your heart and soul. This is why you place me first Joseph for the Father and I are One, with the Holy Spirit. We have been here since the foundation of the earth! It was the three of us that created everything on this earth and throughout the universe. Man cannot comprehend what our eternal home is like or the fact that there really is a place that exist, where life could be around forever." Jesus's eyes fell on the sash. "Would you like me to wash out the blood from your sash while I check with mother about supper?"

"That is very thoughtful Jesus, but I shall take care of it before I come in for supper." Joseph lifted the ax off the floor and stored it safely on the shelf as he watched his special son walk away. He glanced over to find Simon putting away the double blade hatchet along with all the other tools. Joseph reached for a leather pouch and gently placed the bloodstained sash inside and tied it secure never noticing Simon had stopped to watch his unusual behavior and joined him as he reached for a small chest.

"Father, are you going to put that away soiled with blood?" he watched his father glanced over at him then he dropped down and pushed a heavy matt out of the way, the lifted up a wooden door then placed the chest down inside a small opening, and slid the door back before reaching for the heavy matt. "Father, would you care to explain what you just did? You know that blood will just dry on that great-looking sash and you will never get it washed out then."

"Have you considered the fact that I do not wish to lose any of that sacred blood Simon!" Joseph reached up and touched Simon's right ear. "We can praise the Almighty God that your brother was here this day young man or we both would have been wounded! You, now missing your right ear and me, most-likely laid out at the morgue, my head detached from my body!"

"Father, are you saying it was my brother's blood that saved both of us?" Simon had felt something always different about his older brother Jesus, but, he could never put his finger on what made Him stand out from everyone else. "We are family father. Should not our blood-line be the exact same?"

"Simon, one day you will learn the reason why your brother Jesus is different, but I can tell you His blood is like no other man born, not before, not now, not ever." Joseph removed his heavy apron. "You witnessed for yourself how Jesus caught the ax from dropping down on my head. The sharp blade was driven deep inside both his hands and the blood gushed out. I quickly pulled off my waist sash and wrapped it completely around both hand, hoping to stop the flow of blood, then you startled me with your painful cry."

"I remember looking up just as the leather strap broke loose and the sharp ax hurled dangerously down toward your uplifted neck!" Simon recalled what had made him careless. "I never saw Jesus run to reach you, He just simply appeared in a flash to save you." Simon looked at his father with a new sense of gratitude, knowing how close he came to losing him. "Father, do you realize what might have happen if Jesus had reacted like a normal man? No one, no matter how fast they could run, could have outrun that heavy-falling ax! That is why I grew careless with that hatchet father. I just witness my brother Jesus light up like an angel of God!" Simon stared at the ax, now laying safely on a shelf. "Is that why Jesus is special father, is He really an angel of God?"

"I will say this one thing Simon. Your brother Jesus is something greater that God's angel." Joseph gently touched Simon's right ear. "Soon Jesus will leave us to begin His ministry and many miracles will be revealed to all who hear and see Him. My son, you will learn in time who your brother is and discovery Jesus will save more than just a head or an ear, He will save the very soul of all mankind."

CHAPTER 26

As the carpenter's shop faded away, Jeremiah felt a strong hand touch his shoulder and smiled down at the familiar face of his host. "Well children, now you know where to find another remnant containing the Holy blood of our Savior." Simon's kind old eyes looked with faithful respect at the empty space that was alive moments before with activity and miracles. "The one needing healing through salvation and redemption, might find themselves being drawn here or one of the other many places where the blood of the Lamb awaits."

"So, Uncle Simon, Cassie and I will be shown even more places where the precious blood of Jesus is preserved and for the purpose of healing many others who seek His help through prayers?" Jeremiah reached for his wife's hand. "Once we learn all the locations, will we be led by the Spirit of God to the person seeking help?"

"Young one, you are wise to assume that fact, as it is so, but by means you are not accustom too traveling." Simon started walking back down the path as the young couple quickly followed, uncertain by which form they would arrive at their mission's destitution.

"Forgive me Uncle Simon if I sound ignorant over how Jeremiah and I are to reach the chosen place we are needed to go." Cassie had just exchanged glances with her partner and saw confusion on his handsome face as well. "If we do not drive and the place we're to go is not in walking distance like the boyhood home of Jesus where He and Joanna were, or the carpenter's shop of Joseph we just now witness, then by what other means is there?"

Simon's smile was warm and loving as he stopped to reach back at give Cassie a gentle pat on her pretty face. "I keep forgetting this is not my century but a much far-advanced world now, with many avenues in travel. You must forgive my assumption that life still remains as it did when most people's means of travel was by foot, which was always our family's means of traveling. Except for one small donkey my father used on trips when mother would travel along. Some merchants had horses with carts, and the wealthiest people boasted of the finest stallions and larger carts." Simon chuckled and resumed his walk. "You may recall how Jesus walked many dusty roads with his twelve and besides a boat ride or two, brother Jesus had a ride on the family donkey when a toddler and rode into Jerusalem riding the colt of a donkey." Sadness filled Simon's blue eyes, recalling everything that happened to Jesus and he needed to reflect on assisting the young couple placed in his charge. "Your form of travel as redemption missionaries for Jesus Christ will be completely new to you. No form of wheels will take you there, nor any kind of animal. The only walking you will do is after you have been delivered by the Holy Spirit, through the rays of light casting down from the spiritual white dove." There was a twinkle in his warm eyes. "In other words, you will faithfully travel by the light of God after you have finished learning where all the remnants have been preserved."

"I believe the most of the remnants are scattered in and around Jerusalem, where our Savior lost most of His precious blood." Jeremiah had gotten his own healing at the cross on which Jesus died. "I also believe Mary, the mother of our Lord, must have preserved her mourning clothes she wore at her son's crucifixion. She had to be covered with His blood when they laid Jesus's lifeless body in her arms."

"Such a loving mother." Simon had a faraway look on his ancient-looking face. "Her treasures of Jesus were many and among them was the black mourning dress and headcover, soaked by the redeeming Blood of the Lamb of God." Simon quickly noticed the sadness on the young couple's faces and he gathered a hand of each. "Now, be not sad for Mother Mary, for she is happily living with her Son in heaven as well as her beloved Joseph and their beautiful children. Brother Jesus had a massive rose garden waiting for Mother Mary, whose smell filled the air with ten-times the beautiful scent she had loved on earth."

Smiles had returned to the Mitchell's when they reached

the old cottage where Memmi's home cook supper filled the air with a heavenly aroma. Jeremiah couldn't help but think the loving couple were giving them a celebration meal as Memmi kept bringing out her special recipe dishes while Simon kept everyone's glass filled with his homemade wine. They ended the night with Jewish singing and happy dancing, and lots of strong hugs and kisses before they all went to their rooms for the night.

Cassie climbed in the bed as she observed her husband staring at the door, still seated removing his shoes. "Jeremy, I just bet you are thinking the same thing I am thinking."

Snapping out of his thoughts, he finally noticed his wife had already put on her nightgown and climbed in the bed. "I have been trying to figure out what we have been celebrating with Simon and Memmi. I do believe that dear lady made every dish she knew. I am so stuffed with her great cooking, I'm not sure I shall ever fall asleep."

"I have never known Uncle Simon to offer more than two glasses of his terrific wine before." Cassie picked up her book after lighting the candle by their bed. "I lost count after five refills."

"And what's up with the traditional Jewish dance and songs?" Jeremiah pulled on his pajama bottoms. "Those two could have continued celebrating all night I believe." He gave a soft chuckle. "They almost appeared as though they were growing younger the more they sang and danced. They only stopped when they noticed me find a chair and collapsed on it, totally exhausted from the long day."

"Now that you mention it darling, they did appear to have more energy than both of us and the more they celebrated the more youthful they appeared." Cassie stared at her book and laid it back on the bedside table. "Jeremy, maybe we just had one too many refills and with the constant dancing, we just imagined Simon and Memmi growing younger." She watched Jeremiah crinkle his forehead, considering her words. "Could we just be tired and are imagining things?"

Jeremiah gave a nod and climbed in bed yawning. "Mrs. Mitchell, since I cannot come up with another logical reason, our being exhausted and stuffed like a turkey anxious to find a hiding place from the farmers wife's table, I will except your explanation as gospel and try to sleep off this very unusual celebration." Jeremiah pulled Cassie in his arms and slid them down under the cover. "Things will look different in the morning sweetheart, after a goodnight's sleep."

So, Jeremiah and Cassie finally drifted off to sleep never realizing things really would look different in the morning.

CHAPTER 27

Cassie opened her drowsy eyes as her senses picked up an old familiar aroma. She slowly sat up on the side of the bed as not to disturb her sleeping husband. For a few minutes Cassie wondered if she might still be dreaming. The pretty American had not had a descent cup of coffee since leaving the homeland and there was no doubting that rich aroma smell of French Roast.

"I will not know if I do not go and investigate where this heavenly smell is coming from and what Memmi is making that smell exactly like coffee." Cassie thought as she slipped into her robe and slippers and tip-toed to the bedroom door and cracked it open, expecting to find the room in a mess like everyone left it before saying goodnight.

Looking out into the big den as the first rays of dawn filtered through the closed shutters, Cassie gasped out at what she saw. Not only was the large room tidy and showed no sign of a table filled with half-eaten food, the several empty bottles of Simon's homemade wine and their empty glasses they left scattered about, had completely vanished. As the stun young woman walked passed the massive fireplace, a blazed in a-warm-glow-hours before, showed no sign of a previous fire. There was no sign of the large pile of ashes that had accumulated since she and Jeremiah had arrived. The fireplace was clean and shiny.

"By the looks of this room, I'd say Uncle Simon and Aunt Memmi stayed up all night cleaning and now Memmi is busy making breakfast that smells like coffee." Cassie had not seen her husband walked up behind her until he spoke up, causing her to jump.

"Cassie sweetheart, what makes you think my uncle and Memmi spent the night cleaning?" Jeremiah's eyes hadn't grown accustomed to the dim light but his nose had picked up the aroma of fresh brewed coffee, same as his bride. "I awoke and found my girl missing and the scent of French Roast in the morning air so I assumed you woke up, found our host still in bed and went to the kitchen to search for any sign of coffee, found some and boiled us some."

"You, my charming mate, are no where close." Cassie was happy for his company after all the strange happening since she awoke smelling what had to be coffee. "I too smelt coffee that brought me alert. After realizing it wasn't a dream, I put my slippers and robe on and peeked out the door to find the big den dark and vacant of both family and our leftover mess from last night." She reached up for a kiss before adding. "As for whatever spells exactly like coffee, I haven't set foot in the kitchen yet because my detective mind is trying to solve a mystery related to this big room."

"What sort of mystery Cassie can top seeing the past come to life over and over again?" Jeremiah gave her a handsome smile as he anxiously waited, the need to get a cup of that good smelling coffee.

"If you could light one of the lanterns on the mantle while I open a couple of the shutters over the windows, I can show you why I am concern." Cassie walked to the closes window and unlatched the shutter and pushed it open when she heard her husband speak out.

"Where did those two lanterns go and what happen to Memmi's weaved rug that hung down from the ceiling over the mantel?" noticing silence from his wife, Jeremiah glanced over to find her examining a dark walnut table with a crisp-white tablecloth adorning it, and a large bowl of fresh flowers in the center. "he hurried over beside her. "Cassie, what happen to the old harvest table that set here?"

"Jeremy, I assure you, I haven't a clue how that lovely old table was replaced with this one anymore than I can explain who removed the seating pillows for that" Cassie turned him around to face the spot they had all sat the previous night, and pointed to the plush sofa with matching chairs. "very large white sofa and matching chairs!"

As daylight drifted through the big room, the couple could tell everything from the old room had vanished, now replaced with more modern furniture. The fireplace mantel held a beautiful clock and on either side of it set framed pictures of Jeremiah and Cassie's wedding day. The large painting over the mantel revealed why they had been sent there. It was a real likeness of Jesus, the Son of God, crucified on a Roman cross. Once they both saw the title of the painting, they knew they would soon be ready to begin. The title below the painting written in old script: REDEEMED BY THE BLOOD OF THE LAMB.

Hearing a chime go off in the kitchen, the Mitchells glanced at one another before Jeremiah took Cassie's hand and started walking toward the closed door. He slowly opened it only to find it empty of their host. The couple looked around, both stunned at what lay in front of them, a modern kitchen with a cook stove, wall oven, large refrigerator, several small appliances, and one large coffee maker. There was no sign of Memmi's old kitchen. The old brick oven had been replaced with the large wall oven. The large clay water bowl had been replaced with a large double sink. Memmi's crude cookware made from hammered tin, wood, and clay, were no longer hanging nearly on the old pegs next to the dried herbs, a variety of savory flavors that compliment her favorite dishes.

"Jeremiah, it appears everything that belonged to Memmi have vanished. Those lovely old pegs are gone along with all Memmi's old cookware and those delightful herbs that scented up the old kitchen." Looking around slowly, Jeremiah's pretty wife had hoped she would spot at least one familiar thing belonging to the dear lady she had grown to love. "The wooden bowls, utensils, and mugs no longer set next to the wash bowl next to Uncle Simon's leather bag of homemade wine. Cabinets now hang on either side of the double sinks, above a marvel countertop with drawers below it."

"I admit it was a shock to me as well Cassie darling to fine all of Memmi's things replaced with modern appliances but I am delighted to know the coffee maker is not just an elution." Jeremiah gave Cassie a wink when she laughed softly before searching the modern cabinets for coffee cups or mugs. Before she could pull down two china cups, she noticed a tray set-up behind the great smelling coffee.

"It appears someone knew we preferred coffee over herbal tea, like we have gotten every morning since we arrived here." She pulled the tray out, holding three cups, cream in a matching pitcher with the sugar bowl, rounded off with sugar cubes. Cassie carefully lifted the pot to pour in the cups but paused, her mind still confused as to what was going on around them. Jeremiah noticed her hesitation and walked over, took the heavy pot from her hand and sat it back down.

"Darling, is there some sort of problem with the coffee? You seem to be distractive."

"Jeremy, I just cannot wrap my mind on what happened between the time we said goodnight to Uncle Simon and Memmi and got up this morning to a different time." Cassie took his hands. "Is it possible we could be having the same dream?"

"Not likely Cassie, considering everything else we have witness since arriving in the Holy Land." Jeremiah's attention fell on the third cup. "I believe whoever plans to join us for coffee this morning may be able to explain what the devil is going on here."

"And you would be exactly correct Jeremiah Mitchell." Came the familiar voice of the shell lady as she stood smiling in the open back door holding a handful of fresh-cut flowers. "Since you both seemed to be worn out with Simon and Memmi's farewell party, where I heard each of you danced the night away after feasting on Memmi's fine Jewish dishes, popular over 2,000-years-ago, and your Uncles Simon's popular homemade wine, taught him by his elder brother, same time period, I could only assume you two would be sleeping in this morning."

"My dear Fran, surely you do not mean Uncle Simon and his charming wife were just ghost from the past?" Jeremiah felt Cassie take his hand so he held it steady. "And how can you explain their furnishing being from the same period?"

"Not to mention how they just vanished between last night's goodnight and our waking up and taking the past with them." Cassie needed answers to make sense of the sudden change. "Besides, if they were ghost, explain how we could feel their warm-loving hugs and sweet kisses goodnight."

"The explanation is very easy to understand, especially for both of you since you have been witnessing the past come to life again and again." Fran smiled when they glanced at each other, recalling all the times they had witnessed that very thing. "Time can erase many things young ones, but to be a part of the Lord's family makes you more than just immortal beings dwelling in Heaven. Simon Jesu returns to earth to welcome in the new witness of the Redeeming Blood Missions and see that he, Jeremiah along with his wife Cassondra is ready to take over the powerful job."

"Fran, please tell me, is Uncle Simon the same Simon we watched almost cut his ear off in the carpenter's shop and this eldest brother you spoke of, was our Lord and Savior, Jesus Christ?" Jeremiah felt numb, finally realizing the story he had been told as a child about his mother being related to Jesus was actually true, just as Uncle Simon revealed to him and Cassie. "This is why I always burned with the desire to become a minister and preach the salvation of Jesus, my redeemer!" Cassie could only stare at the man she had fallen in love with, knowing the same blood from Mary that ran through Jesus now ran through her Jeremy.

"Now when you remember your ancestral grandparents, Simon and Claudia, he is your grandfather, not your uncle, like your people referred to him as. You will recall the striking resemblance between him and the younger Simon working alongside of his father Joseph and Jesus, in the woodshop, some 2,000-years back." Fran poured three cups of steaming hot coffee before carrying the tray to the small table by the large kitchen window.

She took her seat before motioning them over. "Let us enjoy our coffee, each other's company and this beautiful morning blessed by our Holy Creator." As they took their seats smiling over the great aroma they had missed. "Cream and sugar may be stirred in, if you prefer, now that yesteryear has passed and a more modern area has arrived."

"This coffee is excellent Fran." Jeremiah had fixed his

coffee the way he enjoyed and savored the wonderful flavor. "Although I did enjoy Memmi's hot boiled tea, the American in me prefers a great cup of coffee in the morning." Still smiling, Jeremiah gave her a wink. "Will you be staying with us now that Grandfather Simon has returned to wherever they go when they leave?"

"Oh, I am just filling in for Miss Tilly until she returns from Bethlehem to resume her fantastic job here." Fran laughed softly as she watched to small sparrows fly up to a nest where four little baby birds stuck their heads up, mouths wide open.

Cassie had been watching Fran's interest in a nest of birds when she recalled an unsolved mystery concerning the real Fran Tatum. If this angelic Fran vanished again, she might never know what happened concerning the Sacred Cross being on her when Jeremiah met her on the beach. Then the sudden appearance of the Blue Royal ring on her left finger the day Jesus joined her and Jeremiah as one.

"Fran, could you help me clear up the mystery of how both the Sacred Cross and the Blue Royal ring managed to be taken off the real Fran Tatum's dead body after being buried since 1760?"

"I would be delighted to share just how the poor dead woman's missing jewelry left her from the grave." Fran had a twinkle in her eyes as she shared the story. "The actual fact is that there never was a real-live human lady named Fran Tatum. The Lord asked me to visit the earth as a maker of special heavenly jewelry from the sea and he gave me instructions for three special pieces, blessed by heavens shells with stones, to make them with. Jesus sent me down into the 1700s and had me appear to age as the years passed by. I continued making beautiful shell jewelry as the Shell Lady's popularity grew at Marsh Cove.

"I am Fran, God's Angel, and it was one of his talented Angel artists that painted my picture as the shell lady, to hang in Fannie's Gift Shop. When I appeared to die at a ripe old age, my friend Fannie placed the real heavenly pieces on me, the Sacred Cross around my neck and the Royal Blue ring on my finger, before the coffin lid was closed. As those poor old graveyard workers tossed that dirt down over my fine wooden coffin, filling up my six foot hole, I simply floated up invisible passed them knowing those poor souls were burying an empty coffin. I had sent the third piece up with Jesus, the heart necklace he placed over your head in the Jordan River." Fran smiled over as Jeremiah, listening closely. Your beautiful heavenly gold wedding band with the cross inlay, was created by Jesus, your kinsman and Savior.

"Fran, I have a question of my own for you." Jeremiah recalled the early morning service on the beach Fran had told him about. Did Jesus actually appear on the beach on the Sabbath at sunrise to speak?"

"Jeremy, do you think I would ever tell you a fib? There was a twinkle in her glowing eyes. Jesus did arrive at sunrise so all the gathering angels working below on earth could be refreshed with his perfect love and peace." Fran gazed back at the window at the baby birds being fed by mama and papa bird. She glanced upward and smiled.

"I see Lord." The couple glanced at each other when the loving angel conversed with her Maker. "Yes, your Highest, I am aware what these precious sparrows are teaching me what to do next with—" Fran smiled over at the interested couple before replying— "your precious children before they finish their training." She gave them a wink. "Feed them their breakfast, then show them the last reverent places where your redeeming blood awaits, then watch them fly from their nest, ready to start your mission."

"As always, you are correct Fran." Jesus appeared and smiled at the young couple. "After seeing Mother Mary's two bloodstain treasuries, both her head wrap, where she soaked up my blood at the Roman whipping post where I was tied and flogged 40 times and her black robes she wore at my crucifixion, then held my dead-bleeding body in her arms. Where my dear friend Joseph wrapped me before placing me inside his own tomb, the two women who wiped my brow when I fell near them while pulling the heavy cross. The men who divided my bloodstain cloths while I hang dying and the young servant boy who cleaned the two flogging whips. The

Captain of the soldiers who realized I was indeed the Son of God and asked for the crown of thorns placed over my head. The young lad that quickly gathered up the nails that pierced my hands and feet and Mal'chus, the young man whose ear Peter cut off in Gethsemane went out after dark and got the cross-bar, where the hands where nailed." Jesus opened back the curtains so Jeremiah and Cassie could see the sparrows feeding the young.

"Once you witness where these redeeming keepsakes are, then those needing redemption will start coming to you, led by the spirit. You need not call for guidance as to which sacred spot to take them my beloved, you will simply know and quickly appear to give them aid." The Lord reached for their hands. "Jeremiah, you have already proved your ability to do the work laid out for you. First while in Capernaum, down on the banks of the Sea of Galilee when you helped the old fisherman to find salvation by answering all his unspoken questions he had concerning me. Was this Jesus really the long-awaited Messiah, the Son of God? My son, through your testimony he has now converted many of his fellow Jews by both your words and those spoken by the prophets of old, that led him to believe. While in Capernaum you gave new hope to those fellow Christians watching and listening and they too received the gift of hearing their New Testament come to life by hearing the disciples great catch out in the sea.

Second, you led your own father down another path so he could choose his destiny for a second time. With your mature faith, even in the body of his ten-year-old son, Harvey Mitchell could finally face his demons, turn from them and return back to me.

Because I chose you to be my Redeeming witness of the Sacred Cross, you now have the gift of speaking in tongues, to ensure those from places beyond your native language, you are my chosen. Along with Cassondra, your beloved wife and partner, you shall live a long rewarding life. It will please you to know your mother and father too, have been chosen to preach the gospel at my church here in Jerusalem. Family is always a blessing and joy to have close by, to share the blessed gift of beautiful children." Jesus turned them toward the open window to see the family of sparrows, who now had their attention on their heavenly Creator.

Jesus sang to the sparrows and they flew through the window and landed on his outstretched hand. "Just as the sparrows know their Creator's call, you too shall know it, and lead the lost, the sick, the sad, the blind, deaf, cripple, and all who seek to be redeemed and find salvation." The Lord blew gently on the birds and they sang Him a song then flew to their young.

"Soon my children, you will become like the mother and father Sparrows and fill your own nest with four young ones. There shall be both time to raise your children with much love and training as well as bring hope to the less fortunate and hurting." Jesus reached out and touched them. "Always remember, I am just a prayer away, beloved and I truly love you." The Lord vanished with Fran, leaving the couple along to rejoice.

"My darling Cassie, this day has had many surprises and I am so ready to get on with this beautiful life we have chosen." Jeremiah Mitchell took his beautiful wife in his strong arms and kissed her. "I know what we are to do now my love."

"Then, would you care to share it we me darling." Cassie had never been this happy in her entire life because she had felt the same message as her husband, she just wanted to hear him say it to her. "Tell me what's on your heart and see if it matches mine."

"My beautiful Cassie, we are to start our new life by building our little nest and fill it with our love." Jeremiah lifted her in his arms. "Mama bird, are you ready to fill our nest with precious babies?"

"I would love to start our family while we start our glorious mission for our Lord and Savior, Jeremy." Cassie wrapped her arms around Jeremiah's neck as he made his way back into their very modern bedroom.

Jeremiah whispered after their beautiful-passionate love making. "Now that we have made our first baby, we can prepare for the first soul who needs to be REDEEMED BY THE BLOOD OF THE LAMB!"